"I believe a literary classical work can be defined as dealing with a particular social situation or theme; but it teaches a universal lesson and conveys permanent truth about mankind and human nature in a moral world. When Yiri's published works are evaluated in the given context, they are seen not only as classical literature, but they also provide the techniques as well as the social transformation and spiritual renewal that constitute the quintessence of literature."

Prof. Isaac Barko Lar
English Department, University of Jos.

BLINDNESS OF THE MIND

Blindness of the Mind

No one is Useless

Pusonnam Yiri

AFRICA CHRISTIAN TEXTBOOKS

2015

Blindness of the Mind

© 2011, 2015 by Pusonnam Yiri

Africa Christian Textbooks (ACTS)

ACTS Bookshop, International HQ, TCNN,
PMB 2020, Bukuru, Plateau State, 930008, Nigeria
GSM: +234 (0) 803-589-5328; E-mail: info@acts-ng.com
Website: http://www.acts-ng.com

ISBN: 978-978-905-221-9 Print
ISBN: 978-978-905-256-1 ePub
ISBN: 978-978-905-257-8 Mobi

For further information, contact: 08105397509. Email: pusonnamyiri@gmail.com

DEDICATION

To the ministry of reconciliation to God.

CONTENTS

Introduction 1

Chapter 1 3

Chapter 2 13

Chapter 3 25

Chapter 4 37

Chapter 5 47

Chapter 6 63

Chapter 7 73

Chapter 8 85

Chapter 9 109

Chapter 10 119

Scriptural References 129

ACKNOWLEDGEMENTS

I am deeply grateful to God for His grace to write this book.

I thank my wife for her love and contributions in proof- reading the manuscript. I appreciate our children for their understanding. I am grateful to my parents for their love and training to me.

I thank my editors: Androcules Murray, Janet Dann, Ishaku Kubga, Rev. Jerry Faruk, Dr. Chentu Dauda Nguvugher and Dr. W. Paul Todd for their inputs. I am also grateful to Pastor Allen Tanko for his contribution.

Furthermore, I thank ACTS Management and Board, Daveco, Joseph G. Kadiya, Nihuma Takwi, Mr. & Mrs. Yusuf, and all the people that have contributed to the success of this project.

I also thank my sisters, brother and all co-workers in ministry.

INTRODUCTION

Everyone can become better.

Slavery of the Mind has different faces. Blindness of the Mind is one of them. God's Word says, "They are darkened in their understanding and separated from the life of God because of the ignorance that is in them due to the hardening of their hearts" (Ephesians 4:18 NIV).

Frustration is a major cause of setback in our lives. Some have committed suicide because of it. Some have developed hypertension. Others have engaged themselves in criminal activities, alcoholism and other risky lifestyles.

The idea of salvation is the one of God seeking to save "prostitutes." By prostitution, I mean people who have gone astray from God into slavery to sin.

What comes to your mind anytime you see a drunkard, prostitute, drug addict, prisoner in a prison yard etc? Do you think they are useless? Common sense will easily conclude so. However, when deep thoughts are involved, in line with God's purpose for the world, the fact is that NO ONE IS USELESS. With Jesus, anybody can become a useful vessel for God's glory.

Furthermore, you are to expect more books in the Reconciliation Series by the grace of God. I invite you on board as one of the faithful readers of the books.

I hope by reading this book you will find the answers you have been looking for.

"In him was life, and that life was the light of men."

—John 1:4 NIV

CHAPTER 1

Smoke filled the room as if someone was cooking with firewood, except that the odour was not ordinary. Felicia, a beautiful and young woman of twenty-eight, who was tall and dark in complexion lay on the bed with a male customer, smoking marijuana, which they called 'ganja.' Business recently was good for her. She had suddenly become the envy of other prostitutes in the brothel. Her one room apartment was well furnished with electronic gadgets. The room had only one bed of family size. The clothes in her wardrobe were neatly hung.

"You are scaring me with the way you take this 'ganja,'" Murinji, a huge tall man with a scar on his forehead said with a smile.

"That is why people call me the queen of 'ganja,' or have you forgotten?" Felicia quickly replied, as she smoked more.

Murinji laughed. "That is my girl. That is why I always love to see you."

Felicia suddenly kept quiet.

"Why the sudden change of mood," Murinji asked.

"I have a problem."

"You know you can count on me. Tell me what is wrong with you," Murinji assured.

"My mother called me few hours ago asking me to send some money for the school fees of my younger ones. They would be resuming to school next week."

"How much do you need? Money is not my problem," Murinji boasted, as he removed a bundle of five hundred Naira notes and displayed it before Felicia.

Felicia smiled. "Forty thousand Naira is okay."

Quickly, as he smoked more 'ganja,' Murinji counted out forty thousand Naira and gave it to Felicia. "Don't be afraid to share your problem with me. I am equal to the task."

Felicia jumped out of bed dancing. She held the money with her right hand and smoked 'ganja' with the left hand, thanking Murinji for his generosity.

Suddenly, a customer knocked at Felicia's door. Felicia heard the knock, but refused to open. The man asked other prostitutes that were sitting outside.

"Is Felicia the only person here? Do we look like Felicia's secretaries?" Tigana, a short and fat prostitute responded angrily.

"It is not my fault if you don't enjoy your business. Don't talk to me like that!" the man reacted.

"What will you do? Do you think we are all here to only watch one stupid girl prosper? If you think you are a man, open your big and dirty mouth and ask me of Felicia again. Call me a bastard if I don't slap you!" Tigana said harshly.

"Slap him and see what will happen to you! You ugly good for nothing prostitute," Felicia interrupted, as she opened the door and stormed out of the room.

"You called me ugly?" Tigana asked.

"I did! What can you do?"

I will teach you a lesson you will not forget!"

"You better find another business to do. You are history. Even a mad man will not patronize you here!" Felicia said.

Unexpectedly, Felicia received a slap on her cheek from Tigana. The two prostitutes fought each other like wounded lions, while the other prostitutes cheered them on. It took concerted efforts of Murinji and some other male customers to stop them.

"I will show you the difference between enmity and friendship. You will never know peace in this place!" Felicia warned.

"You can't do anything to me! I will always rise up against you!" Tigana responded angrily.

Kuyanga, the leader of the prostitutes, came to the scene and asked Felicia and Tigana to come to her room for a meeting.

The meeting did not last long. It didn't take Kuyanga time to warn them of their irritating behaviour. She advised them to live in peace with each other for the betterment of their businesses, or she would report them to the manager of the hotel and ask him to give their rooms to other prostitutes on the waiting list.

Felicia and Tigana left the room after the meeting without uttering a word to each other.

Marka, a close friend to Tigana in the brothel followed her to her room. "Did you allow Kuyanga to make peace between you and Felicia?" she asked.

"I am sure you know that will never happen. Felicia must regret her actions. I will deal with her in a way she has never imagined!" Tigana reacted.

"Don't worry. We would make our move at the right time and prove to her that we have been in prostitution first!" Marka replied angrily.

*

Nachau sat in the parlour thinking. Akio his wife walked in and sat by him on the settee.

"You have been quiet for some time. I hope there is no problem?"

"I am just wondering why I have a strong burden to lodge at the Karaki Hotel, considering the nature of the place."

"How is the place?"

"Based on my findings, the place is a combination of a hotel and a brothel."

"I am sure God will help you understand the reason behind your lodging in the hotel when you get there."

"I can feel that it is more than just a writing project."

"For how long will you be away, my dear?"

"I am hoping to finish the revision of the first draft of the book in one week, by God's grace."

Ndatam, Nachau's youngest daughter, was also in the parlour listening to her parents' discussion. "Daddy, please buy me something very special when you are coming back," she requested.

"I will not forget, my dear. To forget your request is to forget myself," Nachau replied his daughter with a smile.

"I hope you can finish the revision in less than a week. We don't want to miss you for a whole week," Akio said.

"I hope my time will be well spent. If I can finish in less than three days, I will certainly be happy, because I have already started missing you people."

"I will pray that you finish in two days, Daddy," Ndatam said.

"I hope God will answer your prayer with a miracle," Nachau remarked, as they walked out of the house to the car, getting set for the journey.

Throughout the journey, Nachau had not stopped thinking about his family. They brought him so much joy. If it had not become necessary for him to spend time alone, free from domestic interferences in order to concentrate on writing a book, he wouldn't have left his comfort zone.

Nachau and his wife have two children. The first is a boy, named Mijah. He was a boarder, in a secondary school at the time of the trip.

Immediately Nachau arrived at the hotel, he checked in. It was his habit to pray whenever he checked into a hotel room, in case the room had been used for dubious purposes. After praying, he kept his laptop on the table and his bag on the bed, as he got ready to take his bath. The hotel was far from quiet. There were people making noise, and loud music not very far from his room.

He still wondered why he had chosen the hotel for his mission, but he was comforted with the fact that his time and steps were not ordered by himself.

The hotel had seven detached flats, with fifteen single rooms in a straight row, directly opposite the flats. The prostitutes in the brothel lived in the single rooms. The hotel management had designed it this way to attract their customers to what the prostitutes had to offer, in order to boost patronage of the hotel. Nachau's flat was close to the rooms of the prostitutes.

Having taken his bath, he went into the restaurant/bar to eat. The place was not convenient to him. He met some people already seated enjoying some delicacies and drinking beer. Nachau sat down and gave his orders immediately the waiter came to him.

"That looks like a new guy in the net," Felicia said to Anano, pointing a hand towards Nachau. Their table was not far from his.

"He came in today. I saw him when he arrived," Anano explained.

"He is handsome. He must be my catch," Felicia stated.

"I had plans for him the moment I saw him," Anano disclosed.

"The job belongs to the fastest," Felicia responded, as she stood up quickly to Nachau.

"Mistress of the game," Anano said teasingly.

"That is my name."

Anano smiled as she continued to eat and watch the game Felicia was playing.

"Hi," Felicia greeted. "Can I join you to reduce your stress?"

"The seats are meant for everybody," Nachau replied with a smile, as he welcomed Felicia to his table.

"I am Felicia," she quickly introduced herself.

"I am Nachau Turomale."

"You must be new here."

"I came in today."

The waiter came and kept on the table, what Nachau had earlier ordered.

"Do you care for something?"

"A bottle of beer will do," Felicia answered quickly.

"I will enjoy your company better if you choose something different."

Felicia kept quiet for awhile, wondering what kind of person Nachau was, because most men that eat in the restaurant\bar enjoyed buying beer for them. "Get me some juice," she finally requested.

Nachau smiled, as he began to eat.

"Why don't you like beer?" Felicia asked curiously.

"It causes many problems."

"What are the problems?"

"You mean you don't know?" Nachau asked.

"It makes a person drunk. Is that your point?"

"That is the least of what it can do."

"What do you mean?"

"A man slept with a goat after getting drunk," Nachau said.

Felicia listened attentively.

"Another drove his car into a ditch, and became paralyzed as a result."

"But a person doesn't have to be drunk," Felicia remarked.

"Not drinking is the first step to not getting drunk."

"What is your room number?" Felicia asked, trying to change the topic of their discussion.

"Room 6."

"Can I pay you a visit tonight?" Felicia asked seductively.

"Maybe another time will be better. I will be very busy settling down tonight."

"I need to compensate you for your drink. It is a waste of money to buy a drink for a beautiful lady like me for nothing."

"I will definitely take advantage of it someday, but not today."

"They say 'time waits for no one,'" Felicia emphasized.

"I will wait for time, since it can't wait for me."

"You are saying that I am not beautiful if you don't let me visit you tonight."

"Time makes a person appreciate a woman's beauty better. That is why I asked for it. If you don't mind, I need to go and rest," Nachau said politely, after eating his food.

"I live in room 2, in case you change your mind," Felicia stated.

"Thank you for the information. I am glad to meet you. See more of you," Nachau said, as he walked away.

"Mistress of the game, how did it go?" Anano asked Felicia, as she joined her where she was.

"There is something about this man that I have never seen before."

"Man is man, there is always the right method and price for getting any of them," Anano encouraged.

"I will get him, whatever it takes!" Felicia exclaimed proudly.

CHAPTER 2

The next morning, Nachau came out of his room and stood outside admiring the view of the beautiful flowers in the hotel premises. Suddenly, he saw Felicia coming out of a black car and walking to her room. She was looking exhausted.

Nachau greeted her with a smile from a distance, but she was not in the mood to respond in like manner.

Quietly, she walked to her room, opened the door, and entered.

Nachau only stood and watched her in silence. As he was about to enter his room, he heard a call. When he turned in that direction, he saw Felicia approaching him.

"Why did you refuse my offer yesterday?" Felicia asked furiously.

"Is that why you did not reply to my greetings cheerfully?"

"It is one of the reasons. You made me look cheap. No man has ever turned me down!"

"Why are you into this type of lifestyle?" Nachau asked, as he avoided her argument.

"I need an answer. Please, don't pretend that you don't know what I was talking about!"

"It is better we start from the beginning. Why are you here?"

Felicia kept quiet for awhile. "You have no right to ask me such a question. "

"But I have a chance."

Felicia forced herself to smile. "It is a long story," she replied sadly. "I am not ready to talk about it now. Maybe another day," she added.

"I hope I will be around when you are ready."

"When are you leaving?"

"In a few days' time."

"I promise to tell you later in the evening."

"I will be willing to hear your story," Nachau said.

Felicia became quiet.

"I avoided your offer yesterday because you were too special for such an offer," Nachau explained.

"What do you mean?"

"Groundnuts are enclosed in shells for a purpose. I prefer to add, rather than to take away."

"You are still confusing me," Felicia responded.

"A story is told of 'a goat that found itself dealing with a big problem because its owner was ill. If the owner died, there would be a funeral, and if he recovered, there would be a thanksgiving service. Both occasions would require meat.'"

Felicia smiled.

"How would you advise the goat to handle the problem?"

"I don't have an answer."

"Will the goat be considered wicked if it prays that its owner should neither recover nor die?"

"If that will help the goat to stay alive, I see no wickedness in its intention," Felicia answered.

"Are you sure?"

Felicia nodded.

Nachau smiled. "I rejected your offer yesterday to keep something alive in you and me," he explained.

"You mean I am dirty, and you are clean?"

"Do you know what makes a rooster to grow to full maturity in a house?"

"Good feeding of course," Felicia answered quickly.

"The best answer as someone observed is the 'patience of the owner of the rooster.'"

Felicia looked surprised.

"Christmas, New Year and other festive periods come and go, but the owner of the rooster would rather buy meat from the market than kill his rooster. A wise rooster should knock at the door of its owner every morning, and thank him for the chance to live," Nachau emphasized.

Felicia looked at Nachau curiously.

"In the same way, we all live because of the mercy of God, our owner."

Felicia stood still, thinking over the lesson in the illustration. Her mind was in turmoil. The power behind Nachau's words was forcing her into thinking seriously about her life, but she was not ready to face reality. Suddenly, Murinji drove into the hotel in his car and called her.

"Excuse me, please. Let me attend to someone," Felicia said, trying to avoid Nachau.

"Feel free to go. We will meet later. There is a saying that 'for the sake of a good relationship, it is not proper for water to cook fish,'" Nachau said.

As she walked away, she stopped, and listened to the proverb. She could not avoid smiling over it.

Murinji, who had overheard the proverb, also became curious. "What does he mean by that proverb? It is interesting."

Felicia kept quiet.

"Who is that guy?" Murinji asked.

"He calls himself Nachau. He is a well of something I feel I am about to discover," Felicia replied, as she walked into her room with Murinji.

*

In the afternoon, after much writing, Nachau decided to leave his car at the hotel, and hired a taxi for sightseeing to refresh his mind.

The driver of the taxi looked worried and hardly smiled. The trip was uninteresting, because of the attitude of the driver.

"I am Nachau Turomale."

The driver did not reply.

"Did you hear what I just said?" Nachau asked.

"My name is Selemo," the driver replied reluctantly.

"You don't look too good."

"I am okay, sir."

"Looking okay has its signs. I have not seen any of the signs on your face."

"My daughter is ill. She was admitted to the hospital yesterday. I don't have money to buy drugs for her," Selemo disclosed.

"How much do you need?"

"Six thousand Naira," Selemo quickly answered.

"Let us go and see her."

"I can't go now, sir, until I raise the money."

"You don't have to worry," Nachau encouraged.

Selemo looked at Nachau calmly.

Nachau and Selemo went to the hospital. On reaching there, Selemo's wife, Usilari, quickly came to him. "Her condition is getting worse. The doctor insisted that we must get the drugs or there is nothing they can do to help her! Did you get the drugs?" she asked anxiously.

"I couldn't get enough money for the drugs," Selemo replied, almost in tears, as he walked to the bed of his daughter to see how she was. "You will be okay, my dear," he assured her.

The doctor came on his medical rounds, and saw Selemo. "Did you get the drugs?" he asked.

"I am still in the process," Selemo responded.

"I don't think you are a serious man. Your daughter is in a critical condition, and you still don't do much to help her."

"Doctor, please, don't talk like that. I have tried my best. Kindly give her the drugs, I will settle up with you later," Selemo requested.

"Please, doctor, help us!" Usilari also begged.

"We don't have the drugs in the hospital. It wouldn't have been a problem if we had them," the doctor remarked.

"Doctor, my name is Nachau Turomale. Kindly give this girl every possible treatment she needs. By God's grace I will settle the bills."

Selemo and his wife looked at Nachau in amazement.

"Take this twenty thousand Naira and hurry to get the drugs, and anything else you know she needs," Nachau said, as he removed the money from his pocket, and gave to Selemo.

Selemo took the money. He and his wife remained speechless for some seconds. "Thank you very much for your kindness, sir," Selemo stammered with tears in his eyes, as he ran out of the ward with the prescription paper to buy the drugs.

"We are really grateful, sir," Usilari said. She too was in tears, as she knelt down before Nachau in appreciation.

"You don't have to do that. Please, stand up. It's all for God's glory," Nachau stated.

Usilari stood up slowly, wiping her tears with the edge of her wrapper and sat on the bed beside her daughter, who was watching the situation.

"Cynthia, Mr. Nachau has given money for your drugs and promised to pay your bills," Usilari said pointing at Nachau.

"Thank you, sir," Cynthia stated faintly.

"I wish you well," Nachau responded with a smile.

"Thank you," Cynthia replied.

"How old is she?" Nachau asked Usilari.

"Twelve years old."

After some minutes, Selemo returned with the drugs, wondering about the kind of person Nachau was.

After the drugs were administered, the doctor assured them that she would get better. Nachau prayed for the girl, and together with Selemo left the hospital for his hotel room. On the way, Nachau engaged Selemo in a discussion.

"Do you like this job?"

"I have no choice, but to like it," Selemo replied.

"If you had a choice, what would you choose to be?"

"I am a professional barber. I want to have my own shop, and employ people to work for me."

"What stopped you from doing that?"

"I don't have the money to start."

"You have the money, what you don't have is the right idea of how to start. Do you know that mountains await those that will tap their potential?"

Selemo kept quiet, as he listened to Nachau.

"Don't be like football players."

"What do you mean, sir?"

"They are limited on the pitch by lines."

Selemo smiled, as he thought over Nachau's perspectives on life. "I have brothers and sisters that could help me, but they are reluctant to do so."

"It seems you are angry with them?"

"I am! They only like giving me a little amount that will not help me start a good business."

"A young lion was pampered by its parents. It had never known hunting experiences. One day, as it was playing with a young antelope, it ran to its mother and cried that it was hungry. The mother looked at it, laughed, and said, 'My son, that little antelope you played with, is food,'" Nachau narrated.

Selemo listened with interest.

"You will lose important experiences of growth when you depend on others for your progress. Do not look into other people's pockets before you face future challenges."

Selemo nodded in understanding.

"Is this your car?"

"No."

"How much do you give the owner daily?"

"One thousand five hundred Naira."

"And how much do you get for yourself?"

"It depends on the patronage. Sometimes I get one thousand or one thousand two hundred Naira."

"Make a business card. Give your card to any passenger you pick up from today. Encourage them to call you whenever they need taxi services from their homes. Once they call, you have succeeded in expanding your circle of people, who will one day become your customers, directly or indirectly in your future barbing business."

Selemo listened attentively.

"When you get home today, write your vision of the kind of saloon you need, and the items you need to start the saloon with. Then begin to see your taxi job as a channel of raising the money for the opening of your saloon."

"I am grateful for all your assistance. You really are an angel."

"It is better you see me as a man. A friend you met today."

"I don't feel like working today. I want to stay with you and listen to your words of wisdom."

"Words are words. They become words of wisdom when they are put into action. Like air in a ball, some people perform better when they are trapped. Use your situational entrapment for growth. Working in addition to listening makes better sense."

Selemo looked at Nachau in deep contemplation.

"You should get an ice cube when you get home. Put it in a cup and watch what happens to it. Tell me of your experience when you come to pick me up tomorrow."

"What is it all about, sir?" Selemo quickly asked.

"Don't be in a hurry. Simply do as I have asked."

"I will certainly do it."

Immediately they reached the hotel, Nachau alighted. "How much is your fare?"

Selemo smiled. "You don't have to worry, sir. After all that you have done today. I am the one that owe you."

"God only used me as a friend to support you, but not as your customer. I will be glad if you allow me to pay for the service, so that you can be on the road tomorrow," Nachau insisted.

"Pay three hundred Naira, since you insist," Selemo replied reluctantly.

Nachau gave him one thousand five hundred Naira. "I know you've undercharged me."

Selemo took the money with some hesitation, "Thank you."

Nachau smiled.

"What time do you want me to come tomorrow?"

"3pm is okay. You can take me to the hospital to see your daughter."

"I will be glad to do that, "Selemo quickly replied.

CHAPTER 3

Nachau sat in the room at night writing. He was in a creative mood, which made the flow of writing easy. He had a cup of tea on the table by his laptop, which he sipped from time to time.

Akio called.

Nachau quickly picked up the phone and answered. "I really miss you, my dear."

"I really miss you too. How are you doing?" Akio asked.

"I am doing fine with the book project. I hope you and the children are doing okay?"

"We are okay. I visited Mijah yesterday. He really missed the family."

Nachau smiled. "I will see him when I return. My mission at the hotel is developing in other ways."

"What are the other ways?"

"I met a lady by the name of Felicia. She is one of the women that live in the brothel."

"You mean a prostitute?" Akio asked quickly.

"Yes."

"I hope she will not try to snatch you from me?" Akio joked.

"You sound afraid of losing me," Nachau replied teasingly.

"Any woman who has a charming husband like you lives in fear for the rest of her life."

"Instead of being afraid, I advise you to pray for me."

"I will do both," Akio laughed. "I am grateful to God for giving you to me as my husband."

"I am more grateful, my dear."

"The Lord will be with you on this mission. Maybe Felicia is one of the reasons for you lodging in the hotel."

"I believe so. I also met a taxi driver named Selemo."

"I am sure God will unfold His purpose for you as you progress. I wish you well. I have no doubt that you are in the right place at the right time. Your love for God is always a challenge to me."

"Thank you for your encouragement as usual."

"I will wait for your call."

"Expect it soon," Nachau replied happily.

After the discussions, Nachau remained quiet, reflecting on his lovely relationship with his wife.

Unexpectedly, he heard a knock on the door.

"Who is it?" he asked, but nobody answered.

The door was knocked again.

Nachau stood up, and opened the door. Felicia was standing outside, dressed in mini skirt and a singlet.

"Hi," she greeted seductively.

Nachau stood speechless looking at her.

"Can I come in? I am curious to know the meaning of the proverb you told me earlier."

"I will explain it better when I join you outside," Nachau said, as he shut the door behind him, and walked out to meet Felicia.

"I will not talk to you outside. I insist we go in, or I will shout, tear my clothes and accuse you of rape. I am sure you don't want that stain on your integrity!" Felicia threatened.

"I am like the fish in that proverb, and you are like the water. Partnering with fire to cook me will not give you the peace you are looking for."

"Do I look like a person looking for peace?" Felicia asked furiously.

"You don't have to tell me about your desire for peace. I know it. Only those who are down have the privilege of pulling others down with them. You are a special lady, Felicia. Add to the blocks of joy, don't take even one away!"

Felicia was calmed for awhile. "I am sorry; I don't know what came over me. I felt miserable that you have not responded to my attractions!"

"I was attracted, but not in the way you had wanted. There is a saying that 'when a bird perches on a rope, neither the bird nor the rope will rest.' My avoidance of your attraction is to enable both of us have a steady rope."

"Who are you? Where have you come from?" Felicia asked in confusion.

"My business is helping people discover the purpose of life for reconciliation to God."

"Are you a Pastor?"

"Just like you, I am a tool in the hand of my Creator."

"What do you mean?"

"Maybe when you've told me your story of how you came here, I will explain what I mean better."

Felicia became quiet for some seconds. "I completed my O' level education eight years ago. I had obtained six credits out of the nine subjects I sat for. Since then, I have tried to get admission into a university to study industrial design, but was rejected because I do not have a credit in English language. I wrote the exam five times, but still was not successful."

Nachau listened with keen interest.

"As an alternative, I learnt tailoring to survive, because my mother is a widow, and I have four younger ones in school to support. Eventually, I rented a shop and started a tailoring business in Abuja, but the shop was demolished. The Government claimed it was not in the city master plan. I didn't know what to do after that. I was forced by circumstances into prostitution." Felicia narrated. "You were right to say I am looking for peace," she added faintly.

"It is really a sad story. I have also been a victim of the 'English language frustration,'" Nachau responded.

Felicia looked at Nachau with surprise.

"I have an opinion that I strongly believe will help raise legitimate response to the problem."

"I need to know your opinion, sir. It may give me the hope I have been searching for."

"This is not the right forum for that."

"Please, I need to hear it."

"I will tell you since you insist. My focus for now is on English language. It should not be on a throne in a village that is not its own."

Felicia listened.

"Insistence on passing English language in our educational system, for admission into tertiary institutions helps some to learn the subject, but to many, it is like forcing a kangaroo to run on four legs," Nachau said.

Felicia nodded.

"Even though the exam method of assessing students is good, it may not be the best. We must learn to consider those who have the strength, but are without arms when we ask people to lift a heavy stone. "

"I completely agree with you, sir. I am academically better than most of my friends, yet they have already finished their university education. I must confess that it is very frustrating for me to sit at home because of English language, watching my friends when they return home on holidays. I often feel inferior."

"When a doctor prescribes a drug to a patient, no matter how good it is, if it causes terrible side effects that can lead to worse problems than the disease in focus, a good doctor changes it. The truth of the matter is that insistence on passing English language before admission is granted is one of the major causes of crime in our societies. What do you expect of a young person who stays at home for some years, waiting for English language to set him free for admission?"

Felicia listened attentively.

"The pressure also leads students to devise ways of cheating, and with these attitudes they grow into leadership in the nation and abroad. The government should find a way of relaxing the tension on the subject. After all, many that passed it on paper cannot practically use it well."

"But will your suggestion not affect the standard of education drastically?"

"It will, but by creating a new standard. Someone shared with me a story of 'a man and some women in a canoe that was loaded with fire wood, and crossing a river. The man paddling the canoe suddenly saw a snake among the woods. If he informed the women, they would panic, and possibly drown in the river. As the best option, he kept quiet until they reached the shore.'"

Felicia listened thoughtfully.

"Common sense will make the man attempt killing the snake in the canoe, but wisdom urged him to deal with the situation otherwise. The goal of every decision should be to save, not to inflict havoc."

"How I wish we would have people like you in our educational systems," Felicia commented.

"Diverse languages are models of the blessings of diversity. Letter 'A' appears more times than other letters in the word 'Adamawa,' but no matter what letter 'A' does, even if it is repeated a million times, it cannot spell 'Adamawa,' it must need the other letters: D, M and W."

"Sir, I can spend a whole day just listening to you."

"In a similar way, salvation is also an exam. The main subject is your relationship with Jesus. You have to answer 'Yes or No,' because we are all guilty of sin, and deserved death because of it. Jesus paid the price for us through His death on the cross and resurrection so that we would have life everlasting."

Felicia became restless.

"If you accept Him as your Lord and Saviour, you will certainly be admitted into fellowship with Him and be free from the bondage of sin."

"Felicia," a customer interrupted with a call. "I will wait in your room, don't waste time please," he added impatiently.

Felicia stood in silence.

"A man is calling you. Maybe we could talk later," Nachau said.

"I am busy. Go to someone else," Felicia announced to her customer.

Nachau was happy to hear that.

"I can't wait," the man replied

"I said I am busy!"

"Okay, I will never come to you again!" the man walked away to meet another prostitute.

"Why didn't you go to him?" Nachau asked, trying to confirm Felicia's interest in their discussions.

"'There is a time for everything,'" Felicia responded.

"You sound like a Holy Bible student."

"I used to be a committed Church-member. I even became the youth fellowship president in our Church," Felicia explained.

"It is never too late to change direction. Odour doesn't last forever when it rises," Nachau encouraged.

Felicia kept quiet.

"Do you like what the Government did by demolishing your shop?"

"I still hate the Government for that!"

"You should hate yourself more."

"What do you mean?"

"The business you are doing now is another form of demolition. But this time, it is worse than shop demolition."

Felicia looked at Nachau keenly.

"It is called the demolition of the mind and body. You are the driver of the demolition machinery. That is why I refused to partner with you in demolishing yourself," Nachau explained.

Felicia remained silent for some time. Tears ran down her cheeks, as she looked up to Nachau. "You must be an angel sent by God to me."

"You still have some blocks left. You can rebuild before it is too late."

"It is not easy to do that. I am already decayed," Felicia lamented.

"God is a specialist in decay management. A bike without fuel produces frustration in pushing it. Let God fuel you with His love, and you will experience the riches of His potential in you."

Felicia walked away from Nachau slowly with her head bowed.

"Where are you going to?"

"I need some time alone."

"You will never be alone, because God will be with you. Someone said that 'no matter how short a person is, his eyes can see the sky.'"

In silence, Felicia walked to her room, locked the door and fell on her bed weeping.

*

Late in the night, around 11:30pm, Anano went and knocked at Felicia's door, but Felicia refused to open it. Felicia also disappointed some customers who had earlier knocked at the door. She insisted that everybody should leave her alone.

Anano's insistence that Felicia open the door finally yielded a positive result. Felicia reluctantly opened it and went back to bed.

"Mistress of the game, what is happening?" Anano asked.

Felicia refused to talk.

Anano sat on the bed close to Felicia. "Talk to me, my friend. Or are you broke?"

"What do you want? Please, I don't want you to disturb me. I am thinking of many things," Felicia responded.

"Tell me your problems. I am equal to the task!"

"When the right time comes, I will let you know," Felicia said.

"Well, I can't force you to tell me."

"What can I do for you? I want to sleep."

"Sleep should not be part of your programme tonight. There are 'big guys' in the city. They are willing to pay a high price for a night. Pato is here to get us," Anano announced happily.

Felicia looked at her quietly, and covered her face with her pillow on the bed.

Anano was surprised at Felicia's response, because she knew her as a fast mover. "Are you going or not?"

"I don't feel like going anywhere. You can go without me," Felicia answered.

"You dare not miss this opportunity, my friend. They are ready to offer fifty thousand Naira to each of us for one night. If we convince them to keep us for two days, we are talking about one hundred thousand Naira," Anano emphasized.

Pato walked in to meet Felicia and Anano. His job is to organize women from tertiary institutions and brothels for the 'big guys' when they come to town. He has an album of beautiful girls with their photos, and phone numbers for easy selection by his customers. He likes the job because it gives him easy cash.

"What is going on? Our customers have been calling me. Why are you delaying?" Pato asked anxiously.

"Felicia has refused to go," Anano answered.

"Why?" Pato asked.

"Ask her," Anano replied.

"What is wrong with you, Felicia?"

"I just don't feel like going out tonight."

"You have no choice, but to go. Two of our customers have specifically requested you. You will spoil our business if you don't go," Pato explained.

"I don't see how I will spoil the business just because of one night off," Felicia argued.

Pato and Anano begged Felicia until she agreed to follow them. Five of the prostitutes from the brothel went with Pato to one of the highly patronized nightclubs in town.

Throughout their stay there, Felicia was not in the mood to participate fully in the activities. Around 2am, she became restless, and insisted that she would go back to the brothel. Pato, Anano and some of their customers were angry with her, but she remained committed to her decision.

"You can find your own way back since you proved to be stubborn!" Pato shouted at her.

Felicia walked out of the club determined to catch a taxi or motorbike to take her back to the brothel. Anano ran after her.

"Are you out of your senses? Don't you know that it is too dangerous for you to go back alone?" Anano shouted angrily.

Felicia only kept quiet, as she walked away from Anano out of the premises. All her efforts to get a taxi failed. She decided to trek until she found a taxi. Suddenly, through the dark, silent street, she heard strange voices commanding her to stop. When she turned to the direction of the voices, she saw three hefty men rushing towards her.

Fearfully, she ran and shouted for help, but no one came to her rescue. They ran after her and caught her. Despite her begging for mercy, they beat her, and finally raped her. They ran away eventually leaving her lying helplessly beside the empty road with blood on her forehead, as a result of the injury she had sustained.

A few minutes later, police on patrol arrived, and found her. They arrested, and put her behind bars at the station for late outing.

CHAPTER 4

Anano went furiously to see Felicia in her room, on returning to the brothel in the morning, but was told by other prostitutes that Felicia did not return. She peeped through the window of Felicia's room to confirm her absence.

News went round in the brothel that Felicia was missing. Some of the prostitutes stood outside in a group discussing the matter.

"Maybe the useless girl found someone, who took her somewhere for the night!" Tigana said.

"Don't you have human feelings, Tigana? At least be reasonable for once!" Anano reacted harshly.

"How can I have human feelings, when the stupid girl has taken over all our customers? Or do you want to claim that you are not feeling the loss?"

"Money is your only interest in life," Anano stated.

Tigana laughed. "Look at who is talking; or have you forgotten that we are all prostitutes? Can you show me one prostitute who is doing that for charity? You'd better forget about Felicia and concentrate on what the day has to offer," Tigana emphasized.

"You are a disgrace to our unity!" Anano responded.

Tigana laughed in mockery, and went into her room. Anano and other prostitutes stood outside wondering where Felicia was.

Nachau came out of his room, curious to know the reason for the noise he had been hearing. He walked up to Anano, greeted her politely, and asked what was going on.

"Felicia is missing, sir," Anano said.

"How do you know that?" Nachau asked.

"She left us at 2am at a night club in the town, with the intention of returning to the brothel," Anano informed him.

"How sure are you that she did not change her mind, or went away with someone?" Nachau asked further.

"I saw her when she went out of the premises. I am sure she did not go with anybody," Anano replied.

"What made you so sure?"

"Considering the amount of money she left behind at the night club, I don't think anybody could afford to pay more."

"Let us check the police stations around here," Nachau said.

"Okay, sir."

Nachau and Anano drove out of the hotel in search of Felicia. She was not in the first station they checked. On their way to the second, Nachau started a discussion with Anano.

"May I know your name?"

"My name is Anano."

"I am Nachau Turomale."

"I know, sir."

Nachau smiled.

"Felicia told me."

"Do you like your job?"

Anano kept quiet, wondering why he had asked her the question.

"Is my question hard to answer?"

"Yes, sir. Nobody has ever asked me this question."

"Maybe today is the right time for the question."

"I have never met a lady who likes doing prostitution."

"Why are you doing it, since you don't like it?"

"To hurt my husband!"

"What do you mean?"

"I was once married. My husband was unfaithful to me. All my efforts to make him stop proved abortive. Eventually, he sent me away, and married a second wife despite all the challenges we had gone through together in our marriage, before he became the Chairman of our Local Government Area."

Nachau listened with keen interest.

"Since he is a politician, I got involved in prostitution to spoil his political career. It is embarrassing to connect him with a prostitute as his ex-wife," Anano explained.

"There is a saying that 'when you are bathing in a river and a mad man takes your clothes and runs away, you should not attempt to run after him.'"

"Why?" Anano quickly asked.

"'People will think you are the one not in your senses since you run after him naked.'"

Anano listened with interest.

"Maintaining malice is very expensive. When you forgive your offenders, you equip them with the tool of forgiveness for their own future use. You need wisdom in handling issues, not anger."

"There is no wisdom that can resolve this problem amicably."

"There was a time rats were a menace to us in our house. As a solution, I decided to kill the rats by using a fish coated with poison and wrapped in polythene sheet. I dropped it outside their hole so that they could easily get and eat it. I was happy when I eventually noticed that they had fallen into the trap by taking it into their hole. But to my surprise, after some time, they pushed it out of the hole intact without eating it. I wondered what must have happened in their hole. Maybe they met an experienced and wise old rat, who must have advised them very well on what to do."

"Now I understand why Felicia has changed since she met you."

"How long have you been involved in this lifestyle?"

"About two years."

"Has your husband visited you since you started?"

"He came once, in the first month of my being here, and begged me to stop."

"Your husband's silence is a sign that he had put on 'SPJ,'" Nachau said.

Anano looked surprised. "What do you mean?"

"I will explain it after we find Felicia."

"I am curious."

"You don't remove electrical poles simply because the electrical company has switched off the light. You allow them to be where they are, and wait for power."

"You are torturing me with proverbs."

"I am only aiming to help you think."

Anano pointed to the police station ahead of them, which was beside the road. "That is the station over there," she said, as she thought over the meaning of 'SPJ.'

When they entered, they were lucky enough to find Felicia. She was still behind bars. Felicia was happy to see them, but also felt ashamed when she saw Nachau.

"Who is she to you?" the police officer at the counter asked harshly when Nachau inquired about the process of bailing Felicia.

"She is a friend," Nachau replied gently.

"You look a respectable person, how can this useless prostitute be your friend? Are you sure of what you said?" the police officer asked.

"Her name is Felicia, sir. I am sure you have it in your record. Please, don't call her useless because she is not," Nachau responded boldly.

"If this one is not useless, what is she?" the police officer said, pointing at Felicia.

Felicia and Anano watched Nachau and the police officer helplessly.

"People become better or worse. It is just a matter of time. Hair on our heads grows again after being cut off. Don't look down on anybody. The worst sinner today can have a different story tomorrow," Nachau explained.

The police officer kept quiet, as he avoided the discussion with Nachau.

Felicia thought deeply about Nachau's approach to the situation. She was surprised at Nachau's open acknowledgement of her as his friend.

Eventually, Nachau bailed Felicia out. He took her to a clinic, and had the wound on her forehead treated. From there, they went to the hotel together. Felicia thanked Nachau and Anano for their efforts. In frustration, Felicia entered her room and slammed the door.

Nachau also entered his room, powered his laptop, and started working on his book. He called his wife and told her about his involvement in Felicia's case. She encouraged him, and prayed with him for more wisdom.

Felicia took some wraps of marijuana and smoked in desperation, thinking it would help her forget her problems. Soon after that, she lay on her bed weeping. Her eyes had become red.

After some time, Murinji visited Felicia. He knocked several times on her door without response from her. He heard only strange movements in the room. Curiously, he peeped through Felicia's window. To his amazement, he saw Felicia tying a rope on the ceiling fan in her room as she stood on a table attempting to commit suicide.

Murinji shouted her name, but Felicia was determined to end her life. His shouting attracted some of the prostitutes to Felicia's door. Quickly, Murinji forced the door open, ran and grabbed Felicia before she jumped off the table.

"Leave me to die. There is nothing in this life for me anymore!" Felicia shouted, as she struggled to fulfil her wish.

"I will not leave you!" Murinji responded angrily.

"If you don't leave me, I will not regard you as my friend."

"It is better than losing you."

When Anano came to the scene and saw what was happening, she quickly ran and called Nachau. Immediately he got the news, he left his writing and ran to the scene, together with Anano. On arrival, he did not wait for permission to enter the room. He stood close to Felicia without speaking; wondering what was on her mind that made her choose suicide as a solution. The odour of marijuana in the room also got his attention.

"I came to this world unlucky! Why me?" Felicia lamented.

"Don't kill hope, Felicia. Let it live. Its benefits are ahead," Nachau encouraged her.

Felicia continued to cry.

"Committing suicide will not solve your problems, you need to be patient," Nachau said.

"I don't know what to do with my life! The problems are too many for me to bear!"

"God knows what to do with your life, Felicia," Nachau stated.

"I thought it was the only option I had," Felicia responded with guilt in her voice.

"It simply means you trusted the rope to solve your problems better than God. It is another form of idolatry," Nachau remarked.

"I want to talk to you alone, sir," Felicia said, having been quiet for awhile.

"Let us go outside," Nachau responded.

"Okay, sir," Felicia agreed.

When they got outside, Nachau saw some birds on a tree. "Look at these birds," he said, pointing at the birds, "Jesus taught that they neither farm nor store grains in barns, yet God takes care of them."

Felicia listened calmly.

"What really happened to you?" Nachau asked.

"I was raped on my way back to the brothel from a night club, early in the morning," Felicia disclosed after some minutes of silence.

Nachau kept quiet for about a minute, looking at Felicia with pity over her condition. "That was really sad," he finally said sympathetically.

"I shouldn't have gone out of my room that night, but I was dragged out by greed. It was very humiliating to be handled like a cabbage!"

"They raped your body, but don't let them rape your mind," Nachau encouraged.

Felicia looked at Nachau. Tears started dropping on her cheeks again. "Sometimes God seems to be unreachable. If only He had answered my prayers earlier, I wouldn't have become a prostitute!"

"So now you blame God over your problems?"

"He shouldn't have allowed me to come here."

"Prayer is like watering a plant. You can't make it grow; but you can hope for it. When you think God doesn't make any sense, it is because the sense is in the making."

Felicia was still in tears as she listened to Nachau.

"God created you with free will to choose between good and evil, so that you will be responsible for your actions. A friend once informed me that 'the eyes see together, cry together and sleep together, but they have never seen each other. That doesn't mean they are not together.' You have not yet seen God in your situation, but He is here. One day you will understand."

Felicia nodded calmly in understanding. "I often feel lonely and frustrated."

"Loneliness is the absence of good ideas. You can go and have some rest and think over what we have discussed."

"Thank you, sir, for your encouragement."

As Felicia was going to her room, Nachau called her. She stopped and turned to him in expectation.

"Marijuana cannot help. Don't depend on it," Nachau said with a smile."Lidimba," he added.

Felicia stood silently, wondering at the sensitivity of Nachau in understanding issues. "What is the meaning of lidimba?" she asked.

"In my culture, it means 'make progress,'" Nachau replied with a smile. "The engine of a car must first be hot before it can effectively achieve its potential."

Felicia listened.

"No one is useless. Crises may cripple you, but don't let them stop you from walking."

Slowly, Felicia moved away to her room.

CHAPTER 5

As earlier arranged, in the afternoon Selemo came to the hotel to pick up Nachau. When Nachau came out of the hotel premises, he was happy to see Selemo already waiting for him.

"Good afternoon, sir."

"Good afternoon, Selemo," Nachau replied, as he opened one of the front doors of the car, and entered.

"I am glad to see you again, sir," Selemo remarked while igniting the car and driving.

"I am also glad. How is your daughter?"

"She is doing better. She really hopes to see you again."

"I am also anxious to see her."

"I did what you asked me to do!"

"What was the result?"

"The ice cube melted into water. I am eager to know the meaning," Selemo said anxiously.

"Don't let your life be blocked by crises, like the refrigerator does to water."

Selemo kept quiet in amazement, looking at Nachau in appreciation of his wisdom.

"When you trust God, He will one day take you out of frustration and your blocked situation will melt away."

"I am certainly waiting for the day," Selemo remarked, after thinking about what Nachau had said.

Nachau responded with a smile.

Selemo picked up a piece of paper on the back seat, and gave it to Nachau. "This is my proposal for the saloon business."

Nachau received it, and read it. "Your plan is big."

Selemo looked on with expectation.

"You need to start bit by bit."

"Okay," Selemo responded.

"And you need to be specific about your vision. There is a proverb that 'if you pursue two rats at the same time, you may end up catching none.'"

Selemo nodded in understanding.

"Break the vision into phases. Don't move to phase two, until you are through with phase one, because every phase comes with its level of discipline."

Selemo listened with keen interest.

"For instance, you don't need to hire two workers and a cashier at phase one as you have written. Design it in a way that you and your wife can be the workers, so that you can save sufficient money for the next stage," Nachau explained.

"My wife doesn't know how to cut hair."

"She should be the cashier, not a barber. But it is also possible to train her to cut hair."

"It will be hard for me to handle on my own the many customers that would patronize us."

"The first stage is for getting started. Not many people will come. The most important thing is for you to think of customers' satisfaction, and effective ways of saving money. Other stages would depend on the strength of this foundation," Nachau clarified.

The car started jerking and moving slowly. Selemo stopped the vehicle by the road. He excused himself, and got out, taking some tools with him. He carefully opened the bonnet, and checked the plugs. "I am sorry for the inconvenience. We need to see a mechanic."

"It wasn't your fault; there is no need to apologize."

Selemo got back into the car, and drove slowly and carefully to a nearby mechanic.

On reaching there, Nachau found a chair under a tree and sat down, watching the various activities at the garage. Selemo joined Nachau immediately the mechanic started fixing the car.

"Life too has its own challenges, just like what happened to this car," Nachau said.

Selemo listened with expectation.

"You must always have a backup plan in pursuing your vision, or else you will end up with mechanics. Knowledge of what you are doing is very important. We wouldn't have been here if you had learnt how to fix the problem that brought us here," Nachau explained jokingly.

"Are you saying I should train to be a mechanic?" Selemo asked.

"A cat fish found itself in the midst of thorns, and cried to other cat fish for help. When they came, they realized that if they tried to rescue it, they would also be injured. The trapped fish thought of calling a man to help it, but it knew that after being pulled out by man, it would end up in a pot."

"So what happened to the fish?"

"It had no option, but to struggle out of the thorns despite the pain and injuries."

"That was a hard thing for the fish to do."

"Every vision has its challenges. Just like the fish, sometimes everyone needs to be the 'mechanic' of his problems by the grace of God."

"Now I understand."

"I want to teach you the TFTA of life."

"What is the meaning of that?" Selemo asked eagerly.

"T stands for THINK. Through thinking, you know your shortcomings and the need for complete trust in God for everything you need. In addition, if you think carefully about what you need in order to achieve your potential, you will discover that you already have more of what you need than what you don't have. People that think well, do well."

Selemo listened.

"F is for FOCUS. Thinking leads you to a river, but focus helps you to catch the type of fish you need. Focus enables you to use energy well, because you will only spend much energy on things that make you move forward positively. People without focus are like a river on rampage, which causes disastrous flood. Every potential is in a shell. Focus is vital in breaking the shell."

"How do I focus?"

"Focus on God first, by trusting Him fully to guide you, and then God will help you to focus on your vision."

"I got the point," Selemo happily said.

"T stands for TEAMWORK. A person who likes working alone is often selfish. Teamwork leads to collective sharing of ideas, which makes effective growth possible. A tree that rejects the friendship of the ground is on its way to destruction."

Selemo nodded joyfully in understanding.

"The idea of teamwork is also seen in our bodies. You have two eyes, two legs, two hands, two ears, ten fingers among others," Nachau explained, as he pointed a hand at Selemo. "Sometimes a person is lucky to have right team members at first stage, but in most cases they have to be discovered in their raw stages and shaped into the vision."

"Sir, you are expanding my view of life."

Nachau smiled. "The A is for ACHIEVE. Talking about your vision is not enough if it is not achieved. Many people have great ideas, but they lack the courage to achieve them. Achievement leads a person to the next stage of life. Gear one in a car prepares the way for gear two. Some things wouldn't have been discovered without achievement. A piece of wood must first achieve its burning potential before ashes become available."

"I am really grateful for your time. You have motivated me for greatness."

"I hope you will always remember to go through the road of humility on your way to greatness?"

Selemo responded with a smile.

After a few minutes, the car was fixed. They went to the hospital and Nachau encouraged Cynthia. Usilari thanked Nachau for his kindness.

From the hospital, Selemo brought Nachau back to the hotel. Nachau had some time of rest and continued writing his book.

*

Later, Nachau went to the restaurant\bar to eat. Anano came and joined him at his table. He told the waiter to serve Anano with her choice of food.

"I am not hungry, sir. Thank you," Anano said.

"Are you sure?"

"I am sure."

"What about juice?"

"I am only hungry to know the meaning of the 'SPJ' you mentioned in our last discussion."

"Curiosity is the foundation of change. The journey of life is like an uncompleted sentence. It has its complete meaning only in Jesus," Nachau explained.

Felicia walked into the restaurant\bar and came to Nachau and Anano's table. "I knocked at your door several times before someone told me that you are here," she said to Nachau.

"I am happy to see you. How are you doing?" Nachau asked.

"How are you feeling?" Anano also asked.

"I am doing better, thank you all for your concern," Felicia remarked.

"To God be the glory," Nachau responded. "Would you care for something to drink?"

"A bottle of soft drink will do," Felicia replied.

Nachau ordered for the drink.

"What really happened?" Anano inquired.

"I don't want to talk about it now!" Felicia answered.

"I asked because I care."

"I know."

Nachau looked at the friends with pity and keen interest.

"That's okay," Anano replied.

The waiter brought a bottle of soft drink for Felicia.

"Sir, I am still waiting to know the meaning of 'SPJ,'" Anano insisted.

"It means 'Shame Proof Jacket,' Nachau disclosed. "Maybe your bullets of shame stopped hitting your husband after the last time he visited."

Anano kept quiet as she thought over what Nachau said.

"What are you talking about?" Felicia asked.

"It is better you hear it from her," Nachau responded.

"Anano, what does that mean?" Felicia inquired.

Anano remained quiet, as she looked at Nachau worriedly.

Felicia also kept quiet without pushing Anano for any reply.

Tigana and Marka entered the restaurant\bar with two of their customers. Tigana came to Felicia when she saw her. "How are you doing, Felicia?"

Felicia slowly looked up at Tigana. "I am doing fine."

"It is a waste of time to answer this witch! She was very happy over your disappearance. She even called you a useless and stupid girl!" Anano reacted in anger, as she woke up from her sleep of silence.

"What can she do now that you are reporting me to her? Is she not useless?" Tigana responded.

Felicia did not say a word. She only concentrated on sipping her soft drink.

"The only witches here are you, and this good for nothing prostitute!" Marka interrupted, pointing a hand towards Anano and Felicia, as she moved closer to them.

"Outdated prostitutes! Go and find another job and leave us alone! You are only jealous of us because we are young and beautiful. Shame on you!" Anano exclaimed.

"Leave them alone, let us go," one of the customers said to Tigana and Marka.

"Leave us to deal with these idiots!" Tigana reacted.

"You are the idiots!" Anano said harshly, as she stood up to face Tigana and Marka. "It is not our fault that you two are ugly!"

Nachau looked on with pity over the conditions of the prostitutes.

"I am sure your husband married another woman because of your ugliness!" Tigana stated wildly.

"See who is talking. A man in women's business. A woman without a womb is a man!" Anano remarked.

Tigana was struck by Anano's words. Her bitter memory of her past resurfaced. She kept quiet looking calmly at Anano.

"Your secret is open to us, Tigana," Anano commented boastfully, taking advantage of the sudden change in Tigana's mood.

"Tigana, you shouldn't allow her get away with that," Marka stated.

"Anano," Felicia called. "Leave them alone."

"Is that the best you can do? Didn't you hear what they said?" Anano said angrily, as she wondered about what had really happened to Felicia. She used to be the best in returning fire for fire when under attack.

"I heard everything they said. Just let them go," Felicia emphasized.

Tigana and Marka could not believe what they saw and heard. Felicia's approach weakened their courage. They went away to their table in shame, and sat down still looking at Felicia.

"To prevent hot temper, water should avoid having a relationship with an active boiler. A proverb states that 'he who forgives wins,'" Nachau encouraged.

Anano sat down.

"We must be like the ground. We dig it and walk on it, but when we die, it welcomes our bodies home," Nachau said.

"I will never like or forgive Tigana and Marka. They are not human beings!" Anano stated.

"Their case is not a closed chapter. They may one day be helpful to you. Electrical cables relate to each other better when there is power. Let your heart be powered by God's love," Nachau explained.

"God forbid! They will never be of help to me in any way!" Anano reacted.

"A story is told of a lion and a rat. Out of hunger, the lion caught a rat to eat. The rat begged the lion not to eat it because it would one day be useful to it. The lion laughed at it, and attempted to eat it because there was no way a rat could help a lion."

Felicia and Anano listened curiously.

"After many persuasions by the rat, the lion finally set it free. One day, the lion was caught in a net trap. All its efforts to escape proved abortive. Suddenly, it saw passing by, the rat it had earlier let go. The lion begged the rat to help it out."

Anano and Felicia listened attentively.

"'I told you that I would be useful to you one day,' the rat reminded the lion. Eventually, it used its teeth to cut off the net. The lion escaped to freedom as a result," Nachau narrated.

"You are the most interesting man I have ever met," Anano said with a smile.

"I will only be interesting when you act on all the lessons we have talked about."

"It is a matter of time," Anano replied.

"How can I have peace, sir?" Felicia asked.

"You can find peace in Jesus," Nachau replied quickly.

"I have offended Jesus in many ways. There is no way he would accept me back."

"He has never left you. It was you who left Him."

"A prostitute like me has no place in His programme," Felicia said.

"Jesus is a friend of prostitutes; let Him handle your situation. There was a woman in the Holy Bible who lived in Samaria like a prostitute."

"You mean the Samaritan woman?" Felicia asked.

"I am glad you know the story," Nachau said. "Do you remember what happened to her after she met Jesus?"

"Through her, many people in Samaria believed in Him," Felicia replied.

"There was also Rahab, who saved the spies Joshua sent to Jericho."

"It is too late for me now. There is no way I could be accepted into a normal community," Felicia said sadly.

"Even if they reject you, Jesus will not throw you out. He came to seek and save the lost," Nachau encouraged.

"If I accept Him, I am sure you will ask me to leave this business," Anano interrupted.

"That will be left for you to decide. When you cannot cross over the wall of fear around you, it is good to grow taller than it, to enable you see what is behind it. That is a good motivation for crossing over," Nachau explained.

"I don't think I am ready now," Anano stated.

"But He is ready for you," Nachau emphasized.

"Since God is patient, I believe He will wait for me until I am ready," Anano declared.

"There was a time we saw a hen at a zoo, in a python's cage, searching and eating food freely, while the python was having its rest. The hen probably had no idea of the danger around it. After some time, we went to the zoo again, but the hen was not in the cage," Nachau narrated.

Anano kept quiet, as she thought over what Nachau had said.

"No one knows when his earthly journey will end. We must be careful how we live in this world," Nachau emphasized.

"I am really fed up with this life. I really want to believe in Jesus!" Felicia stated.

"Would you like to accept Him now?" Nachau asked.

Suddenly, a young girl walked into the restaurant\bar and announced that Kuyanga wanted to see all the prostitutes in their compound for a meeting.

Anano and Felicia stood up reluctantly. "Excuse us, please," Anano said.

"What about the decision you were about to make?" Nachau asked Felicia.

"We would discuss that another time," Felicia replied gently.

Nachau was speechless for awhile. Suddenly, he became curious about the young girl that announced the meeting. "What is the name of the young girl that informed you of the meeting?" he asked, after the girl had left.

"Her name is Rose," Felicia answered.

"Is she also part of you here?"

"Yes. She is a moneymaking machine for Tigana. She brought her from the village. She lied to her parents that she would help her secure a good job in the city," Anano explained.

"How old is she?" Nachau asked worriedly.

"She is only sixteen years old," Anano replied.

"Thank you for the information," Nachau remarked.

Felicia and Anano quickly left for the meeting.

Nachau was worried over the distraction at the time Felicia was about to make a commitment to serve Jesus. He comforted himself with the fact that God works in mysterious ways.

*

All the prostitutes assembled at the compound. Many of them wondered about the purpose of the meeting.

Kuyanga did not waste much time in breaking the moment of suspense. "It has come to my notice that you have not been meeting the needs of your customers well. As a result, our businesses and unity are affected, especially in the last three days. I hope you have not forgotten that our successes depend on the patronage of our customers?"

The prostitutes looked at Kuyanga quietly.

"Especially you, Felicia," Kuyanga said, pointing a hand at Felicia.

Felicia looked at Kuyanga calmly.

"Some customers complained to me about you. You have become aggressive in your business. What has come over you?" Kuyanga asked.

Felicia still maintained silence.

"I am asking you, Felicia. Don't ignore me like that!" Kuyanga reacted.

"There is no problem," Felicia answered.

"She is lying!" Tigana interrupted.

"Nobody asked you, 'madam big mouth!'" Anano said.

"I am not talking to you!" Tigana replied.

"It's enough! Keep quiet!" Kuyanga shouted.

"I have been thinking of many things recently," Felicia stated.

"Since she met one customer they call Nachau, she has become something else," Tigana explained.

"Which customer?" Kuyanga asked.

"The one in room 6," Tigana replied.

"Is it true Felicia?" Kuyanga inquired.

"It is true that he had contributed, but I have the right to choose how my life should be," Felicia responded.

"You have the right as long as it will not affect our businesses here. Get over whatever is wrong with you, or decide whether you want to remain here or not; and that applies to all of us!" Kuyanga warned.

The prostitutes looked at Kuyanga in silence.

"We are all partners. We can never achieve progress with hatred among ourselves. We need peace and tolerance in this place. I don't want any customer to complain again," Kuyanga said. "Is there any question or comment?" she asked.

None of the prostitutes was interested in asking a question or making further comments.

"You can go. The meeting is over," Kuyanga stated. "Felicia," she called.

"Yes," Felicia answered.

"Don't go, I want us to talk," Kuyanga informed.

Felicia waited reluctantly.

Anano left the meeting venue angry with Felicia for not reacting against Tigana.

Kuyanga further warned Felicia against wasting time with Nachau; describing him as a dangerous guest, who was not after their bright future.

Felicia nodded in approval of what Kuyanga had said.

"You can go," Kuyanga stated.

Quietly, Felicia walked to her room and lay on the bed contemplating her life. For some hours at night, she thought of what to do. Whether or not to quit prostitution occupied her mind.

CHAPTER 6

Earlier, Kuyanga had informed the manager about Nachau's influence on Felicia. The next day at 10am, Nachau went out of his room, as usual, to look around the premises. Suddenly, he saw a male customer coming out of Felicia's room with Felicia.

On seeing that, Nachau became worried. He had thought Felicia was considering quitting prostitution.

He called her when she was returning to her room, after seeing her customer off.

"How are you today?"

"I am doing fine," Felicia answered reluctantly.

"How was the meeting you had yesterday?"

"Please, I know where you are heading. I don't want to talk about it. Spending time with you is harming my business," Felicia quickly remarked.

"Do you know how to use a computer?" Nachau asked.

"Not much," Felicia replied, after being quiet for awhile.

"When you want to delete a file, this question comes up, 'Are you sure you want to move this file to the Recycle Bin?' The options are 'Yes' or 'No.'"

Felicia looked at Nachau.

"Please, don't click 'No,' but 'Yes,' then proceed to the recycle bin and delete it permanently out of your computer, to deny it any chance of restoration. In the same way, our lives have some files that we need to delete. "

"It is better you leave me the way you found me."

"God designed us for progress."

"Our leader was angry with me for frustrating some of our customers since I started spending time with you."

"Every change comes with its consequences. You should not allow anyone to lead you to death."

"I don't think I have a better choice for now, because this is the job that provides food for me and our family. I am not ready to abandon it!" Felicia declared emotionally.

"I understand what you are going through. However, food is not permanent. Some have it, but they lack the appetite to eat. Someone told me of a woman involved in prostitution who became infected with a deadly disease as a result. Before she died, she set her house and belongings on fire so that nobody could enjoy her labour after she died.'"

Felicia looked on thoughtfully.

"Don't gain the world and lose your soul," Nachau explained.

"Nothing good will ever come of me again. I have tried my best!"

"You are almost there, Felicia. Grass struggles for prominence in the hostile world of farmers; but that does not stop it from persevering for progress," Nachau encouraged.

"You don't know what it means to be in my situation."

"I know what it means to be in a worse situation than you are in," Nachau said.

Felicia looked at Nachau in confusion. "What do you mean?"

"Some years ago, I was involved in terrible things."

Suddenly Goddy and Kuyanga came out of Goddy's office after a meeting, where they discussed the issue of Nachau's influence. When they saw Felicia talking to Nachau, they were not happy. Angrily Goddy called to her.

"Sorry. We would continue later. I have to see the manager," Felicia said restlessly, as she moved away.

"A proverb says, 'he who swallows a pestle, cannot sit down,'" Nachau responded.

Goddy frowned, as he waited for Felicia to come to them. "Kuyanga told me that she had warned you about wasting time with that man!" he said, the moment Felicia reached him.

"Yes, she did," Felicia reluctantly stated.

"What are you still doing with him?" Goddy asked harshly.

"Don't make my situation worse. You have no right to control my life. I am trying to do my best to keep the flow of business okay for all of us!" Felicia reacted.

"You better do. No one lives here only for himself. Let me remind you that there are other tenants that are desperate for your room," Goddy threatened.

"Have I ever failed to pay my rent?"

"You have not," Goddy replied.

"Then why are you harassing me?"

"It is not only about your rent. Your activeness makes people to patronize this place. As a result, we have extension of patronage to our other services. You people are like the hunting dogs," Goddy explained.

"All you care about is your personal interest!"

"You have no right to talk to the manager like that. Don't forget that it is because he gave us accommodation that is why we are surviving here!" Kuyanga reacted.

Felicia walked away in anger to the bar, ordered for a bottle of beer, and started drinking.

Goddy approached Nachau for a discussion. "Good morning, sir."

"How are you doing?"

"I am doing okay."

"That is good."

"With all due respect, I beg you to stop distracting our ladies from their assignments. We need their concentration for the development of this place so that we can also have resources to serve you better."

Nachau looked at Goddy with pity because of his display of selfishness. "This place is like an abattoir. The ladies are like your 'cows.' But very soon, by God's grace, you will run out of meat," Nachau responded.

"Are you wishing us bad luck?" Goddy asked anxiously.

"Bad is the state of your hotel. I am only trying to squeeze good out of it. There is a saying that 'your staff will not get hooked on a tree for long, when you make a monkey your friend,'" Nachau replied.

Goddy could not resist smiling. "I don't understand."

"You need right relationships to succeed. The successes you get on the backs of others don't last long. I am not against every aspect of your business. My main concern for now is the prostitution."

Goddy looked at Nachau, speechless.

"When you step on grass, always remember that they are homes to many insects."

"So I need to step on them carefully. Is that what you mean?"

"Yes."

"I support missionary work in my Church, and pay tithe from this business. If it is not right, why am I still succeeding?"

"God doesn't like cheerful givers who give from cheerless sources. Every human being, based on his self-assessment can assume he is healthy, but the doctor's report can prove otherwise!"

Goddy listened attentively.

"I call this type of success of yours 'balloon success.' Very soon, it will reach its limit and then it will explode! The real success is in Jesus. The Word of God says, 'By humility and the fear of the Lord are riches, and honour, and life.'"

A staff member of the hotel suddenly called the manager and informed him that one of their important guests was in his office waiting for him. Goddy told the staff member to tell the customer to give him a few minutes.

Nachau watched the situation with expectation.

"My pastor knows my kind of business; but he has never spoken to me against it. He was the one that dedicated this hotel when it was built before we started operations."

"When you first identify what you have done wrong, it will help you know the type of pastor you have."

Goddy listened anxiously.

"Are you married?"

"No sir."

"When you marry and God blesses you with a daughter, my wish for you is to have your daughter work in your brothel as a prostitute."

"I reject that in Jesus' name!" Goddy shouted. "How can you wish that for my daughter?"

Nachau looked seriously. "Each woman living here as a prostitute is someone's daughter. If you can't wish that for your daughter, then it is time to think about your next line of business."

Goddy kept quiet, thinking about what Nachau had said.

Nachau waited patiently for him to conclude his journey of thoughts.

"You are making me feel guilty, sir," Goddy remarked.

"Guilt is a major raw material for change. Every drop of rain is full of potential."

"I have never assessed my business from your point of view."

"Plants change their outlook before they bear fruit. Maybe that is what is happening to you."

"I am really grateful for your time, sir."

"God will be more glorified when you become a doer of what you have learnt."

"I will think more about it," Goddy replied seriously.

"A drum should not think of itself and forget the hands that beat it."

Goddy listened, as he walked away.

Nachau stood looking at Goddy with joy over the discovery he had made. "God, please let him respond to your love," he prayed.

*

Goddy sent for Felicia to come to his office. When Felicia got the message, she thought over the reason for the invitation. On reaching the office, she knocked anxiously on the door.

Goddy asked her to come in. When she entered, she saw him reading a book. She was surprised because that was the first time she'd ever seen Goddy show an interest in reading.

"You are welcome, Felicia. Please, have a seat," Goddy said respectfully.

"Thank you, sir," Felicia responded, as she sat down thinking about his polite approach, which was not normal. She had known him as a wicked and selfish man in all his dealings, and she had never wanted to cross his path in any way. "I hope it is not about my attitude again?"

Goddy smiled, as he kept the book on the table. "It is not, but about where your attitude has led me to."

"Did you have a discussion with Nachau?"

"How did you know?" Goddy asked.

"It shows on the faces of those that have had conversations with him."

"The man spoke to me like no other. The short time I had with him is turning upside down some of my principles of life."

"I am happy; at least you will now learn to tolerate my new attitude."

"Right now, I don't know whether his arrival in this hotel is a blessing or a curse. I am afraid of what I suspect might happen," Goddy said worriedly.

"He might send us out of business. Is that what you are thinking?"

"That is the point," Goddy quickly remarked.

"We have a choice: to accept what he is saying or reject it. He has no right to impose his belief on us."

"He has no right, but his words are not easily forgotten, and what you can't forget can be a source of change."

"Well, let us see how it goes," Felicia stated thoughtfully.

Suddenly, Tigana walked confidently into the office without knocking.

"Tigana, you are welcome," Goddy said with a smile.

"Thank you," Tigana replied, as she sat down on a chair next to Felicia.

"How are you, Tigana?" Felicia asked politely as a way of greeting.

"Don't waste your time pretending to be nice," Tigana replied harshly.

"Please, don't turn it into an argument again," Felicia responded.

"I don't need your greeting, because you will never have mine."

"You two are always after each other," Goddy remarked.

"May I go now, sir?" Felicia asked.

"You can go. Thank you for your time," Goddy replied.

Felicia stood up and walked out of the office.

"I hope she is not trying to take over my position with you, considering the way you two were discussing?" Tigana inquired anxiously.

"There is no need for fear. Your position is safe. You still remain my favourite business partner among them all."

"Then you have to be careful with Felicia. She knows how to turn happiness into sorrow," Tigana emphasized.

Goddy listened.

"I came to tell you that you should not buy lunch today. As usual, I will cook a delicious meal for you."

"That is nice! You always know what I want," Goddy responded with excitement.

Tigana smiled.

"I hope later you will also visit me at home?" Goddy asked.

"That's a good idea."

"Looking forward to seeing your delicious meal," Goddy said.

"I will not waste time," Tigana assured him, as she stood up to go.

CHAPTER 7

Nachau saw Tigana on her way to the restaurant\bar. He called her to talk to her.

Tigana came to Nachau and greeted him respectfully.

"How are you doing today?"

"I am doing fine, sir," Tigana answered. "I hope there is no problem?"

"There is," Nachau replied.

Tigana looked at him in expectation.

"I want to talk to you about Rose. I hope you would not mind?"

Tigana's mind became restless. "Is there any problem with Rose?"

"I learnt that she is here because of you."

Tigana was silent for awhile. "I know that Felicia and Anano must be behind this."

Nachau kept quiet and looked at her with expectation.

"My answer to your question is yes," Tigana replied. "I hope you are not here to tell me that it is wrong?"

"Do you have any good reason for doing that?" Nachau asked politely.

Tigana spent some time thinking on the question.

Nachau did not push her hard for an answer. He waited patiently for her response.

"I did it to achieve my goal of hurting all parents because of what my parents did to me!"

Nachau became surprised.

"I became pregnant as a teenager. I was expelled from secondary school. My father sent me out of his house despite many people begging him to forgive me. With no place to go to, I went and stayed with the man responsible for the pregnancy. He convinced me to abort the pregnancy. Eventually, the pregnancy was aborted, but I was left with the greatest loss in my life."

Nachau listens attentively.

Tigana started sobbing. "I lost my womb as a result. Few weeks after that, the man I was staying with sent me packing out of his house. I had no option, but to join prostitution."

Tears filled Nachau's eyes, as he listened to Tigana's story. "What happened to you was challenging," he said.

Tigana continued sobbing.

"You cannot make progress by living in the past. You must first hurt yourself before hurting someone else. You should please reconsider your goal before it is too late."

"All parents do not deserve good daughters. You don't know what it means to pass through what I have passed through. I was treated without mercy. Now I am only a woman by name. I will never have a family of my own. You were there when Anano insulted me. All these happened to me because of my parents' wickedness. You have no right to tell me to reconsider my mission. Parents have not yet seen the worse of me. I will introduce more young girls into prostitution!" Tigana reacted furiously in tears.

"Rose doesn't have to pass through what you had passed through. You can use your experiences to help, not to destroy."

"With all due respect, sir, I need to go. I have something important to do."

"Thank you for your time," Nachau stated.

Tigana moved away in tears.

Nachau stood and looked at her as she moved away. "Heal Tigana, Lord, from the injuries of her mind. Set her free from bondage and let her see the light of true salvation," Nachau prayed silently.

*

Tigana called Rose because a male customer had asked for her to spend the weekend with him in his house. When Rose came, Tigana informed her of the arrangement. Tigana had charged him fifteen thousand Naira. The man had already paid the money in advance.

"Aunty, I am having severe headache. I really need to rest," Rose said faintly in fear.

"Shut up your mouth! I have already informed you several times that there is no rest in this our business. This is the last time you will complain to me of any problem whenever I am sending you on an assignment!" Tigana responded bitterly.

"I am sorry. I will not complain again," Rose remarked worriedly.

"Go and prepare for the assignment, the man will come back in thirty minutes. He had gone to buy something not far from here," Tigana ordered.

Rose hurriedly walked away to her room.

"Rose, come back! "Tigana called.

Rose quickly went back to Tigana.

"I have something very important to tell you. Since I brought you from the village, are you not happy that at least I have been sending money to your parents from our work?"

"I am happy," Rose answered reluctantly.

"I am sure I have taken care of you more than your parents. You have never slept hungry like you used to do in the village, and you have been wearing good clothes and living in a room paid by me."

Rose nodded in agreement.

"There is a guest in the hotel. His name is Nachau. He often sits and discusses with Felicia and Anano. Have you ever seen him?"

"Yes."

"The man is evil. Don't pay attention to him. He does not have anything good to offer you. He is here to deny us happiness. I will not be happy if I see you with him or hear that you have allowed him to talk with you. I hope I have made myself clear?"

"Yes."

"That is my girl. Go now and prepare for the weekend.

Rose went and prepared her things. When the man came, she went with him to his house.

*

Selemo came to see Nachau in the hotel on a motorcycle. He knocked at the door anxiously.

Nachau was busy writing. When he opened the door, he was happy to see Selemo.

"You are welcome, Selemo."

"Thank you, sir."

"Please, come in."

"Okay, sir," Selemo said, as he entered the room.

"How is your daughter doing?"

"She is doing better. The doctor told me yesterday that she might soon be discharged."

"God is faithful; to Him alone be the glory."

"But there is another big problem."

"What is it?"

"I can't have the barbing saloon again."

"Why?"

"I haven't got the car anymore."

"What happened?"

"The owner retrieved it, and gave it to his younger brother."

"Is that why you are looking miserable?"

"That car, according to your advice, was my only hope."

"A good flask holds hot water. Be like that."

Selemo anxiously looked at Nachau.

"A leader once told me that 'when a flowing river meets a stone, it doesn't withdraw; but progresses through another way.'"

"Life is really miserable!" Selemo lamented.

"Life is like a drum. God uses us as drummers. The sound you get out of it depends on how you use it," Nachau explained.

"In that case, I can say that mine is beating itself."

Nachau smiled. "It is not possible. You have allowed someone to beat it for you. You are only following the sound. That is disastrous," he explained.

"What can I do?"

"What do you have?"

"I have a motorcycle, and some household items," Selemo replied thoughtfully.

"Why have you not been using your motorcycle for commercial purposes?"

"It is too risky to use it in this town. Thieves have been stabbing people with knives in their efforts to steal motorcycles."

"Let us go outside to my car, I will explain something to you."

"Okay."

When they got to the car, Nachau showed Selemo his spare tyre. "People that have spare tyres in their cars are purposeful. They have the right understanding of the reality of having flat tyres on their journeys to various destinations. What just happened to you is like a flat tyre. There is a need for you to have a spare plan for raising funds for your business; but you must first count the cost."

Selemo listened with interest.

"I want to see your 'plan B' for raising funds and your budget."

"Okay, sir. I will work on it."

"There is always a way out," Nachau assured him.

"I am grateful for your encouragement."

"Gratitude is sweeter after a task in hand is completed. Thank you for the visit."

*

Felicia invited Anano at night to come and listen to the story Nachau wanted to share with her about his past life. As usual, they found him at the restaurant\bar drinking some juice.

When they reached his table, they drew out seats and sat down.

"How are you doing, sir?" Anano asked with a smile.

"I am doing fine," Nachau replied.

"I hope you were not mad with me for cutting short our last discussions?" Felicia inquired.

Nachau responded with a smile.

"I am curious to know the story you wanted to share with me about your past," Felicia said.

"My past lifestyle was one of bitterness. While in secondary school, my friends introduced me to hard drugs. As a result, I became a nuisance to my parents and community."

Felicia and Anano looked at Nachau with surprise.

"I was seen as useless by many people. One thing led to the other. I eventually found myself stealing my parents' money in order to maintain my drug addiction. Angrily, my father sent me to a young people's home for rehabilitation. Since I could not get drugs at the centre, I chose aggression as a way of escape from my problems."

Felicia and Anano listened attentively.

"After seven months in the centre, I was finally released with an undertaking that I would be a good boy. However, things became worse two months after my release. I left home, and joined my friends in another state, where we were involved in reckless lifestyles with women who were into prostitution and other things that are now horrible to mention."

"How come you are now like this?" Anano quickly asked.

"I met a former classmate. He talked to me about Jesus. Eventually, I accepted Jesus as my Lord and Saviour. That is why I am like this," Nachau explained.

"You are lucky to have a change of lifestyle," Anano responded softly.

"You can also have yours. It is not yet too late."

"It doesn't work for everybody," Felicia objected.

"It is available for everybody. It depends on our willingness to tap the source," Nachau clarified.

"I am really moved by your story. It's like fiction, considering your present lifestyle," Felicia responded.

"If you make a move today towards change, your story will also encourage someone in the future."

"My situation is very complicated. Leaving this job will mean starting from scratch. I cannot afford the embarrassment that would cause me!" Felicia said in confusion.

"The embarrassment you think you will have will not be new, because I also faced ridicule before people eventually accepted me into community life."

"I am really grateful for your story. You have set me on a long journey of thoughts," Anano stated.

"To have sight yet not be able to see is another level of blindness," Nachau remarked.

"You mean we are blind?" Felicia asked.

"I am saying that the ceiling of every home has something in it that the owner of the house is unaware of," Nachau responded.

A customer came and called Felicia. Reluctantly, she went with him. Nachau was left with Anano.

"If I accept Jesus, that means I have to leave my business. And if I leave, it means that my husband has won the battle," Anano said.

"Proving people wrong is sometimes good motivation for growth. When you shoot at the sky, you should not prepare for it to fall down. The earlier you think of what is good for you the better, rather than thinking of what will give your husband pain."

As Anano was thinking over what Nachau had said, another customer came into the restaurant\bar and called her out. Once again, Nachau was left alone.

He stood up and went to his room thinking of the stubbornness of his friends and their unwillingness to respond to the love of God. On entering his room, he called his wife and shared the situations with her, urging her to pray along with him for good results in his interactions with the women. Akio encouraged him and prayed with him over the phone for God's encouragement. "God will give you victory at the right time and in His own way," Akio declared after the prayer.

"I am sure He will. Thank you."

CHAPTER 8

Selemo was heading to the hotel on his motorcycle to see Nachau. Felicia, who had gone to the market for shopping, stopped him. "I am going to Karaki Hotel," Felicia said.

"Fifty Naira," Selemo responded.

"I will pay forty Naira."

"Let's go."

As soon as they left for the hotel, Selemo engaged Felicia in a discussion.

"I have been visiting a friend at the hotel."

Felicia kept quiet.

"His name is Nachau," Selemo continued talking, as he ignored Felicia's avoidance of the discussion.

"I know him," Felicia said reluctantly.

"He is a very good man. My life has not been the same since I met him."

"I am not surprised. Improving people is his business," Felicia stated.

"Did he also get to you?"

"His life is like perfume, a person feels it even without him talking."

"I am on my way to see him."

"Meeting him has put my life under pressure," Felicia remarked.

"Pressure for good, or bad?"

"I think he meant well, but my fear has succeeded in building a fence around me."

"Would you lose anything if the fence is broken?"

"You are beginning to sound like him," Felicia said with a smile.

"A person cannot swim in a river without it touching his body. I am half way to destroying my wall of fear since I met him."

"I want to, but I am afraid of the snakes I will encounter, since my wall is old."

"What do you mean? You are also beginning to sound like him."

They both laughed.

"I am ashamed to tell you that I live in the brothel as a prostitute. I fear what happens if I abandon the work."

"Is that the best you can do with your life?" Selemo asked, after thinking for awhile.

"For now I am really confused. I know this lifestyle is not for me."

"I am happy you chose to share your life with me."

"I don't know why I told you," Felicia quickly said.

"We are all travellers on the same road of confusion. I am not into prostitution like you, but I also have my problems. But just like Nachau tried to inform me, I know there is still hope for me."

"You don't sound like a commercial motorcyclist. You have a way of relating well."

"I became like this recently. Meeting Nachau has really stretched my mind."

"What are you going to see him for?"

"He shared a method with me on how to raise money for business, and asked me to bring my plan and budget to him today," Selemo explained.

"I would love to join you people in your discussion."

"I don't think Nachau will find any problem with that."

Eventually, they reached the hotel. Felicia disembarked and gave Selemo the money.

"Don't worry. You don't have to pay, since we have become friends," Selemo said.

"Are you sure it's okay?"

"I am sure."

Both of them entered the premises of the hotel. Selemo waited for Felicia to drop her things in her room, and together they went to see Nachau.

After knocking at the door, Nachau opened the door and was surprised to see Felicia and Selemo together.

"You are welcome," Nachau said.

"Thank you, sir," Selemo and Felicia replied.

"Do you people know each other?"

"We met today and became friends through you," Felicia answered.

"I understand. Please, come in," Nachau said.

Selemo walked in, but Felicia remained outside.

"You can also come in," Nachau stated.

"I thought you didn't like it?" Felicia asked anxiously.

"Today is different. We are three," Nachau replied with a smile.

"I understand," Felicia said also with a smile, as she walked into the room.

"Please, have a seat," Nachau offered.

Selemo and Felicia sat down.

"How is your daughter doing?"

"She is responding well to treatment," Selemo replied.

"Is your daughter sick?" Felicia asked curiously.

"Yes," Selemo replied.

"I wish her well," Felicia said.

"Thank you for your concern," Selemo responded.

"Who do I see first?" Nachau asked.

"We are both here for the same reason. He told me about his planned discussion with you. I am here because I am interested. I hope you will not mind?" Felicia explained.

"It is great having you around," Nachau remarked.

Felicia smiled.

"Are you ready with the plan and budget?" Nachau asked Selemo.

"Yes, sir," Selemo replied, as he handed a piece of paper to Nachau.

Nachau took some time to read the paper carefully. "Do you really need two hundred thousand Naira for a start?"

"Yes," Selemo answered. "I have made up my mind to use my motorcycle for commercial purposes. I started today. Felicia was my first passenger," Selemo explained.

Felicia smiled. "No wonder you did not look like the normal commercial riders I know," she said.

"How would you handle the risk involved?" Nachau asked.

"The risk involved is less than the risk of losing my family to hunger, if I don't," Selemo replied.

"It is your decision to make, but I advise you to be careful. Don't be as rough as most of them are if you want to survive," Nachau said.

"I will be careful. It is just for a short time until I get an alternative."

"I hope you have charged Felicia well?" Nachau asked jokingly.

"I charged her well, but we became friends before we got to the hotel," Selemo replied.

"As a result he did not take my money," Felicia commented.

"Why didn't you take her money?" Nachau asked.

"I felt the new relationship we had developed is better than money," Selemo answered.

"A relationship is very good, but if you handle business like that, how will you raise the money you need when twenty of your friends become your passengers in a day?"

Selemo smiled.

"You cannot save the money you don't have. Friends should even pay more, because your growth is also theirs," Nachau emphasized.

Felicia also smiled. "You are right, sir. I think it is the right thing to do."

"Don't forget that channels of resources are to be serviced, or else they easily develop rust," Nachau commented.

Selemo nodded in understanding.

"How can I also raise some money for my business?" Felicia asked.

"What kind of business do you want to do?" Nachau inquired.

"I want to re-establish my tailoring business," Felicia replied.

"What do you have that you can use as a source of raising money?" Nachau asked further.

"I know you will not approve of what I have," Felicia responded.

"It means you also disapprove of it, since you find it difficult to mention it. A good idea is a source of joy," Nachau explained.

"I knew what your response would be."

"Please, feel free to share it with us," Nachau encouraged.

"Is it okay if I use what I do now to raise money for my business?" Felicia asked.

"You can, but it is better you don't," Nachau replied.

"Why?" Felicia inquired.

Selemo looked on curiously, as he listened to their discussions.

"Your investment will remind you of the source. And by that time you may not like to be reminded of your past," Nachau explained.

"But I have nothing else to fall back on," Felicia objected.

"That is what you think. A parked car does not always mean a faulty one. Let God ignite your potential, and you will be surprised at how far you can go. You won't know how deep a river is from outside," Nachau clarified.

"I have been confused since the day I met you," Felicia admitted.

"Confusion is often a sign of progress," Nachau responded.

"I don't understand?" Selemo asked quickly.

"It shows that you are alive. It also leads you to solutions to your problems if you let it."

Selemo smiled. "You have not yet commented on my budget," he said.

"Two hundred thousand Naira is too much for a start. It is always better to start small."

"I will work hard and manage the money well when I have it," Selemo assured.

"Take my complimentary card. Try to raise the money. Call me after one month, and inform me of how much you have raised," Nachau said.

"Thank you, sir. I will certainly call when the time comes," Selemo stated after taking the card.

"Can I also have your card?" Felicia asked.

"Why not?" Nachau responded, as he gave her a card.

"Thank you. I will think about what you said, because I hate to continue as a slave to prostitution," Felicia commented.

"I can help you understand other types of slavery if you want me to," Nachau said.

"I need to know them," Felicia stated anxiously.

"Me too!" Selemo said.

"Let us go to the restaurant and have some soft drinks. We would discuss further on that," Nachau remarked.

"Curiosity is already getting the better of me," Felicia commented.

All of them stood up and went out to the restaurant\bar. On their way, they met Anano, who was standing and discussing with a man.

"Anano, please come!" Felicia invited.

"Give me some minutes," Anano responded.

"What I called you for is more important than what you are doing," Felicia said.

"Excuse me, please," Anano said to the man she was discussing with, as she walked to Felicia. "What is it?" Anano asked.

"Nachau is teaching us on different types of slavery. I don't want you to miss that."

"Do I look like a slave?"

"You don't look it, but I know we don't want to remain here," Felicia answered.

"That man over there is a big catch, and you want me to lose him just like that?"

"You can have him some other day, or someone better; but Nachau will not be here for long. Let us learn everything we can from him before it is too late," Felicia emphasized.

"Please, don't waste my time!" the man who was with Anano shouted.

Anano turned in his direction. "Give me just a minute," she requested.

"I can't. If you are not ready, I will look for someone who is!" he said angrily.

"Go and look for someone else!" Anano reacted.

"Useless prostitute!"

"Useless man!"

"Let us go," Felicia said to Anano.

They went and joined Nachau and Selemo in the restaurant\bar.

"Good afternoon, Anano," Nachau greeted.

"Afternoon, sir," she responded.

"I invited her to be part of the discussion," Felicia said.

"That is very good. A person should not grow alone. Others must be considered along the way," Nachau explained.

Felicia and Anano smiled.

"This is Anano, my friend," Felicia introduced Anano to Selemo.

"It is a pleasure meeting you," Selemo stated.

"The pleasure is mine," Anano responded.

Nachau ordered soft drinks for all of them. As they began to sip, he started his teaching. "There are many different types of slavery; but we would only look at a few. The first type I want to discuss with you is 'Emotional Slavery'-the inability of a person to maintain good people in his circle of friends who could help him out of slavery, because of his aggressive approach to life. The Holy Bible discourages us from interacting with a hot-tempered person, for we may learn his ways."

"Tigana has emotional slavery," Anano commented quickly.

"If you must assess someone, do it through yourself so that you will also be a beneficiary of your assessment," Nachau advised.

"Sir, Anano is worse at this than Tigana," Felicia stated.

They all laughed.

"The second one is 'Knowledge Slavery'- A slave under this category has ignorance or little knowledge as his master. He rejects anything outside what he knows. Change is his enemy. Many of them have money, but they are confused about how to use the money, because they lack good ideas," Nachau explained.

Selemo sipped his drink, as he listened carefully to Nachau.

Nachau's cell phone rang. "Let me answer it. It is my wife."

"There is no problem, sir," Felicia said.

"Hello."

"How are you, my dear?" Akio asked.

"I am fine."

"I hope you are making progress with your project?"

"It is developing, but gradually," Nachau explained.

"We are missing you," Akio said.

Suddenly, the network failed. Nachau tried for some time to call back, but could not. He decided to send a text message, informing her that he would call later.

As soon as he had sent the text, he returned to his discussion with his friends. "Slavery is like a network failure," Nachau joked.

Felicia and the others smiled.

"It can frustrate you when you least expect it," Nachau added.

"But one has no control over network. The best thing is to keep trying," Selemo responded.

"You are right. Another option is to own multiple cell phones with different service providers. When one fails, you can depend on the others, and when all fail, one may revive faster than the others may," Nachau explained.

"Sir, you are always full of good answers," Anano commented.

Nachau smiled. "Where did I stop on the types of slavery?"

"Knowledge slavery," Felicia answered.

"Thank you for reminding me. The next type is 'Relationship Slavery.' Some people have good ideas and resources, but they don't have good friends who could assist them with advice and implementation. They are enslaved to bad friends and their selfish interests," Nachau stated.

Felicia and the others listened attentively.

"We also have 'History Slavery.' Those who don't know their past history well may find it difficult to work out where they are going. They depend on the history of other people for survival. In view of that, they become second class people wherever they find themselves."

"Are you sure history is that important?" Selemo quickly asked.

"If you don't know how others handled life before, you will miss the joy of making progress. The beauty of life's adventure begins when you discover your identity, which is possible through history," Nachau replied.

Selemo nodded in agreement.

"'Financial Slavery' is also another type. Money is the master in this category. People are enslaved by the love of money. They try to get it by all means so that they could have and maintain high living."

"I think I belong to this category very well," Felicia confessed.

"What are you doing about it?" Nachau asked.

"I will think of a solution," Felicia responded.

"The next type of slavery is of two types: positive and negative. The negative type is the source of all errors. Once you discover its solution, it leads you to freedom," Nachau explained.

Felicia and the others gazed at Nachau silently in deep expectation.

"It is known as 'Spiritual Slavery.' The positive one is slavery to righteousness where pleasing God is the focus, while the negative one is slavery to sin, which is living to please the devil," Nachau disclosed.

The silence deepened. The disclosure hit Felicia and others hard. None of them had expected Nachau to mention that.

"We belong to the negative type," Felicia admitted.

"What can I do to get out of the negative spiritual slavery?" Selemo asked.

"Simply accept Jesus as your Lord and Saviour," Nachau answered.

"It sounds easy," Anano said.

"It is the best decision a person can ever make. The Devil tries hard to ensure that many people are distracted from making this decision," Nachau explained.

"But I still go to Church for Sunday worship," Anano said.

Nachau picked up his cell phone on the table, and pointed it towards Anano. "Some cell phones look good, but they have no batteries. Others have batteries, but they are not fully charged. Some have fully charged batteries, but they have not been recharged with units. Some have been recharged, but no service, while some have all the necessary requirements. Which of these cell phones would be effective in communication?" Nachau asked.

Once again, there was silence for awhile.

"The last group," Felicia answered gently.

"In a similar way, accepting Jesus makes you effective for His use," Nachau explained.

"What you have said has really touched my life," Selemo commented.

"Responding positively is the best option. If you are ready, we can pray," Nachau said, as he also turned to Felicia and Anano, waiting eagerly for their responses.

"I am ready, sir," Selemo stated.

"What about you, Felicia and Anano?"

Felicia and Anano kept quiet as they stared at Nachau.

"So it is true that you live as a prostitute in this town?" a strange voice angrily interrupted the moment. When Felicia turned towards the direction of the familiar voice, like a dream, she saw her mother standing behind her. Tigana had directed the mother to the restaurant \bar when she came asking.

Quickly, Felicia stood up. "Mama, what are you doing here? Who told you that I am here?"

"You are a disgrace to our family. So, all this while, you have been sending us money from prostitution?"

"Mama, it is not the way you see it," Felicia answered.

"You have nothing to explain. You lied to us that you were working in a company."

Nachau and the others only looked in surprise at the mother and daughter.

"Mama, let us go to my room, I will explain everything," Felicia begged in confusion.

"There is nothing to explain. I have confirmed what I was told. Someone who saw you here told me, and gave me your address. I didn't believe him until now. I decided to pay you a surprise visit to see things for myself!"

Nachau looked at the situation with pity.

Felicia was speechless. Tears rolled down her cheeks. She had never expected such a moment.

"I will not waste my time here. I am going. Don't bother to come after me!" Felicia's mother continued, as she walked out.

Felicia rushed after her mother. The mother turned to her and harshly warned her to go back. She threatened to curse her if she persisted.

In confusion, Felicia stood helpless, as she watched her mother walk away. She ran to her room and cried bitterly, thinking of the embarrassment she had caused her mother, because she knew that as the breadwinner, she was the favourite in the family.

She also remembered how her mother had stood up in Church, in their village, and given thanks to God in a testimony, when Felicia had told her that she had a job with a company in the city.

Anano ran after Felicia to talk to her, while Nachau and Selemo stood silently outside the restaurant\bar watching the situation.

Suddenly, Selemo's cell phone rang. He removed it from his pocket and smiled when he saw his wife's number. "Hello, my dear."

"Please, come now to the hospital!" Usilari said.

"What is the problem?" Selemo asked anxiously.

"Cynthia wants to see you."

"I will soon be on my way," Selemo responded.

"Is there any problem?" Nachau inquired curiously.

"Cynthia wants to see me at the hospital."

"I will call you later," Nachau said.

Selemo left the hotel on his motorcycle. He picked a passenger, who was going in the same direction as him. On the way, Selemo was occupied with deep thoughts over different issues of life. Suddenly, a reckless car driver hit the motorcycle of Selemo with his car.

Selemo and the passenger fell off the road. They both sustained bruises on their foreheads and some parts of their bodies. Many people rushed to the scene to help. The driver of the car didn't stop. He sped off amidst shouting by the crowd for him to stop.

Someone quickly came to the scene with his car. Selemo and the passenger were rushed to the hospital. At the emergency unit, they were received quickly for treatment. Selemo was discharged after an hour. He refused to inform his wife in view of the situation she was managing in the hospital with their daughter.

The passenger on his part was not responding well to treatments. He needed further examination. He gave Selemo his wife's phone number to inform her of the situation. Selemo did as he was asked to. The wife screamed when she got the information and started crying. His efforts to calm her proved abortive. Selemo gave her the name and location of the hospital and ended the interaction.

His mind was deeply in chaos wondering about why life was fighting him hard. His eyes were full of tears, as he called Nachau.

Nachau did not waste time to answer the call. Selemo informed him of the situation. He also described the location of the hospital, which was not too far from the hotel where Nachau was lodging.

Quickly, Nachau got ready and went out of his room to his car. As he was about entering the car, Rose ran to him, threw a piece of paper inside his car, and ran away fearfully. Nachau picked it and read through. She only wrote one sentence on the paper, "PLEASE, HELP ME GET OUT OF HERE!"

Nachau waited in silence for awhile after reading the note, thinking of what to do. He raised his head and saw Rose standing afar. She ran away when he called her to come to him.

Eventually, he decided to rush and see Selemo first, then come back immediately and discuss with Rose. He ignited the car and drove out in search of the hospital. When he finally located it, he drove in, parked the car, and asked for the emergency unit.

Selemo was sitting on a chair with bandages on his forehead and leg. Nachau entered the unit and sat beside him, as he asked him of what happened.

Selemo gently explained the situation. He tried to control his tears, as he narrated the story, but he could not. He cried without any hope of light at the end of his dark moment.

"You do not have to complete the story. We will talk later," Nachau said.

"I am finished! Life is very cruel to me!" Selemo stated bitterly.

Nachau kept quiet looking at him in pity over his condition.

Suddenly, the wife of the passenger ran into the unit in desperation to see her husband. On catching sight of him on the bed, she ran to him, held his hand and cried. It took the concerted efforts of the nurses to put her under control.

Nachau gave Selemo some money to give to the passenger as his support for his treatment. The passenger's wife collected it and thanked Nachau.

On the way, Nachau avoided an interaction with Selemo. He wanted him to think deeply and experience inner healing.

"God doesn't care for me!" Selemo broke the moment of silence.

Still Nachau maintained his silence, as he listened to Selemo.

"I came to this world only to suffer. There is no meaning to my life!" Selemo lamented.

Nachau still maintained his silence.

"Problems know only me. This is not ordinary. I am sure someone is after my life."

"All these pieces of your life will one day make sense," Nachau said.

"I am really on the hot side of life. I see no hope at all from this point!"

"Hope sees you. Heat is the price of progress. There is a reason why all these are happening to you my friend."

"I almost lost my life today."

"God saved you for a reason. He doesn't sustain a person that has finished his mission on earth."

"This is the worst moment in my life!"

"Each moment is a ladder that takes you closer to achieving your assignment in life. Letter 'P' is the only problem in the word 'Pain.' When you replace it with letter 'G,' you will have the word 'Gain.'

Selemo kept quiet thinking over Nachau's encouragement.

Nachau waited in silence for Selemo's response.

"My motorcycle was the only source of income I had left. Now it is gone. I am finished. There is nothing I can do to support my family!"

"Is it beyond repairs?"

"From the way I saw it, I doubt if anything good would come out of it."

"Don't lose hope. Some years ago, I also lost some important things in my life. I lost my first job, which I got three years after graduation from the university. After that, the house I rented was destroyed by fire. I only managed to save the briefcase containing my credentials and few other important documents."

Selemo listened.

"It got to a point that I returned to the village to stay with my parents. It was a shameful thing to live with them as a grown up person. I became a laughing stock in the village. As a result of the embarrassment, I started farming for people on their farms for small amounts of money to raise funds that would enable me rent a room apartment in the town where I was staying."

Selemo's attention was deeply involved in the interaction.

"Eventually, I saved some money and rented a room. I also secured a temporary teaching job in a private primary school. The salary was not encouraging. Many people discouraged my would-be wife from marrying me when we were courting, because they believed I would remain poor for the rest of my life. My wife loved me very much. She didn't listen to their complaints. We got married in the end. We experienced suffering after that. We thought God had completely forgotten about us."

"How did you get out of it?" Selemo asked curiously.

"We were encouraged by God's Word. James 1:2-5 say, 'Consider it pure joy, my brothers, whenever you face trials of many kinds, because you know that the testing of your faith develops perseverance. Perseverance must finish its work so that you may be mature and complete, not lacking anything.'"

Selemo listened.

"I got an idea of writing a book. My third book by God's grace became successful."

"Thank you for your story. Let me call my wife."

"It is important you do so."

As Selemo was trying to dial his wife's number, a call came in. When he checked, it was his wife calling.

"Hello, dear," Selemo answered anxiously.

"You need to come to the hospital now!" Usilari said in tears.

"What is wrong?" Selemo inquired, but no further response.

"Is there any problem?" Nachau asked.

"My wife needs me now at the hospital. She was crying on phone."

"Let us rush and meet them," Nachau urged.

On reaching the hospital, Selemo experienced a piercing feeling through his heart.

Usilari rushed to him weeping and rolling on the ground. "Cynthia is dead! Cynthia is dead!"

"What?" Selemo reacted.

Usilari continued to roll on the ground weeping. She didn't even notice Selemo's condition.

Nachau tried hard to put Usilari under control, but his efforts did not yield immediate result.

Selemo left his wife outside the ward and rushed into the ward, where two nurses were preparing to cover the corpse with a blanket. The doctor stood by Cynthia's bed, writing in a file.

Selemo stood speechless beside the corpse watching, as if it was a dream. The sight of her lifeless innocent face broke Selemo's courage. He bent down and held tightly to her body weeping.

Nachau encouraged Usilari, and walked into the ward leaving some people consoling her. "What happened?" Nachau asked the doctor.

"She suddenly went into coma about an hour ago. We tried our best to save her life," the doctor explained.

"I thought she was getting better?"

"Medically, her case had improved before now," the doctor explained.

Nachau left the doctor and went to console Selemo. It took some time before Selemo and his wife calmed down.

"What happened to you?" Usilari asked, after noticing the condition of Selemo.

"I had an accident on my way," Selemo explained.

"Oh my God, why us?" Usilari lamented.

Nachau encouraged them further and eventually settled the bills before they left the hospital for Selemo's house. The corpse was deposited at the mortuary.

CHAPTER 9

The journey to Selemo's village for the burial was rough. The road was not good. Many people, especially from his neighbourhood, went to the village to condole with Selemo's family. Nachau too went with them.

When they got there, they were received amidst weeping sympathizers.

Selemo wanted special treatment given to Nachau as his special guest, but Nachau insisted on being treated just like others.

Later in the evening, after the burial, Selemo got involved in a discussion with Nachau.

"Why did God allow such a thing to happen to us?" Selemo asked.

"God loves your daughter even more than you do, my friend. In a time like this, good reasoning is difficult because of the pain," Nachau encouraged.

"She was our only daughter!" Selemo lamented.

"You got her from God. Only He knew the plan he had for her before she became part of your family," Nachau explained.

"But she was very young!" Selemo responded.

"An old woman came to a man, and begged him to allow her to farm on his piece of land. After due consideration, he approved her request, but with the understanding that he was expecting some money to start building a house on the land. Any time he had the money, he would start the project. The old woman agreed to his condition and started her farm project."

Selemo and the other people around him listened attentively to the story.

"The maize the woman sowed grew well. She applied fertilizer and waited for it to mature. Everybody loved her farm. Eventually, the landowner got the money he had been expecting. Early in the morning, he hired a bulldozer and cleared the land together with the old woman's farm."

Selemo gazed at Nachau worriedly.

"The old woman was angry with him for that. Others criticized him bitterly for his wickedness in not considering the hardship of the old woman and the tenderness of the farm. The questions are, did this man do anything wrong? Was he wicked?" Nachau concluded.

Selemo and others kept quiet for awhile. "Since he had given her his condition earlier, to be honest he had not done anything wrong," Selemo answered thoughtfully.

"God has clearly explained to us in His Word, that we would not live on earth forever. Whether young or old, death is real for everyone. Or have you forgotten that even unborn babies also die?"

Selemo and the others were held fascinated by the analysis.

"Why do we blame God when we lose someone? I know it is not easy, but our attitude should be of trust, and thanksgiving, not of blame," Nachau explained.

"It is just that the experience is very painful," Selemo said.

"I have never lost a baby like you. I can't claim to understand how painful it is, but I can assure you that God is in control," Nachau responded.

Selemo kept quiet, without further expression of bitterness, and concentrated on the other guests who were coming into the compound to greet his family.

*

Later, Nachau stood up and went out of the compound to call his wife on the phone. After discussing with her, he spent some time looking at the beauty of the village. A man named Alte, who was one of the major farmers in the village, came to him.

"Good day, sir," Alte greeted politely.

"Good day," Nachau remarked.

"I listened to your story a few minutes ago," Alte said with a smile.

"Did you enjoy it?"

"Very much. It was as if you were speaking to me, not to Selemo."

"I am happy to hear that. What is your story?"

"I am ashamed to say it."

"Shame is often a sign of growth to another level. Let it make you better, not bitter."

"I used to be an elder in one of the Church denominations in this village. My wife and I lived for fourteen years without the blessing of the womb.

We were very happy when finally God blessed us with a baby boy. He was the centre of everything we did. Many people celebrated with us."

Nachau listened with curiosity.

"Four years later, tragedy struck. The baby became ill and died. As a result, my wife and I became angry with God, and left the Church. We stopped praying and studying the Holy Bible. We went back to worshiping idols in order to make God angry. Different pastors and other people visited us for counselling, but we remained stubborn. We did not even allow them to enter our house. When you were talking, I felt a great burden lifted off my heart. I could not control my tears after your teaching. I went out of the compound and cried bitterly, asking God to forgive me."

Nachau listened attentively.

"I believe God has forgiven me. I have already made up my mind to go back to the Church. I am sure my wife will also understand when I share my testimony with her."

"I am very happy to hear your testimony. Accept my sympathy over your huge loss of the baby."

"Thank you, sir."

"God has many ways of reaching us. Depend on Him always. He will use you greatly for His glory."

"How I wish you would not leave this village. I feel like I have known you for many years."

Nachau smiled. "It is the grace of God that is sustaining us, not because of our own personal efforts."

"Thank you, sir, for the encouragement."

"To God be the glory."

*

The following day in the afternoon, Nachau was ready to leave the village. Selemo and his wife thanked him for his concern.

Alte brought some foodstuff and two live chickens to Nachau as a way of appreciating his friendship. Nachau wanted to refuse the gifts because there was no place for him to keep them in the hotel; but he also knew how much he would hurt Alte if he refused. He thanked him for his gifts and they exchanged phone numbers.

On his way, Nachau saw an old woman carrying firewood on her head, in company with a young man who was also carrying firewood. They looked fragile, as if they had not eaten for days.

Nachau pulled over a short distance away from them, and got out of the car.

"Good afternoon," Nachau greeted them.

"Good afternoon, sir," the old woman replied.

"Good afternoon, sir," the young man greeted Nachau.

"I have few things that I think will be helpful to you," Nachau said, as he opened the boot of his car to get the foodstuff, and the back door to get the chickens, kept on the foot mat. "Please have these."

"You mean we should have all these as our own?" the old woman inquired nervously.

"Yes, all are yours," Nachau replied.

The old woman and the young man quickly put down the firewood they were carrying and gathered up the items.

"God will bless you. We are really grateful!" the old woman said in tears. "You are sent by God to help us. Our foodstuff got finished yesterday. I am a widow. Two of my children died last year, one after the other. Their six children are with me. My intention," pointing at the firewood, "was to beg neighbours for foodstuff to cook for today so that we would not die of hunger," the old woman narrated.

Nachau thought of how many resources some people have and waste, while for some it is a matter of life and death. He took some money from his wallet and gave to the old woman.

The old woman lifted her hands up towards the sky, and thanked God for sending His servant. She held tight to Nachau, still in tears. "May God bless the woman that gave birth to you. May He bless your family and everything you do. May He guide you away from danger that will harm you!"

"To God be the glory" Nachau responded.

A few minutes later, Nachau left the woman and her son. As he drove off, he waved goodbye to them.

The woman waved continuously, as his car got out of sight.

On the way, Nachau thought of the miracle of small things done in love. He asked God to use him always as a blessing, wherever he found himself.

*

After two hours of driving, Nachau reached the hotel. The first person he saw was Tigana, smoking a cigarette under a tree.

"Good afternoon, Tigana," Nachau greeted, as he came out of his car.

"Good afternoon, sir," Tigana replied reluctantly.

"Have you seen Felicia?"

"She went out with Murinji since yesterday."

"Thank you," Nachau said.

Tigana kept quiet, as she continued to smoke.

"I can see that you and Felicia don't get along fine," Nachau stated.

"Felicia is the cause; but your coming here has turned her into a better person."

Nachau smiled.

"I must confess that I have felt guilty in the way I have been relating with her recently."

"Why?"

"She has refused to retaliate despite my negative attitude towards her."

"Maybe she has realized something that you are yet to realize. There is a saying that 'when sandpaper brushes a plank of wood, it becomes worn out, while the wood becomes smooth.'"

Tigana in silence discarded the stick of cigarette she was holding.

"Have you thought over our last discussion about Rose?"

"I did. I promise you that I will take her back home soon," Tigana replied gently, after maintaining silence for a moment.

"I hope you will keep to your word," Nachau said, as he questioned within his mind the commitment of Tigana to her promise. "I will be back after one week of departure from here to confirm your promise."

"You don't have to go to that extent. I will fulfil my promise."

"Thank you. But do you know that Jesus loves you?"

Tigana kept quiet, as she thought over the question.

Nachau left her thinking and went to his room. On his way, he met Anano.

"You are welcome back, sir," Anano said.

"Thank you, Anano. I heard that Felicia has gone out with Murinji."

"Yes, since yesterday."

"I thought she would travel home to reconcile with her mother."

"She also thought of doing that in few days to come."

"That is a good thing for her to do. When is she coming back?"

"I don't know, sir."

"That's okay. How are you doing?"

"I am fine, except that the place is boring without Felicia."

"You have a choice, Anano."

Anano smiled. "I know, sir."

"By the grace of God, I hope to be on my way home tomorrow morning."

"We would certainly miss you."

"You will not miss me if you remember our discussions."

"I hope to always remember."

"I need to go to my room."

"Thank you, sir, for everything."

When Nachau got to his room, he prayed and thanked God for safe trip. He also prayed for Selemo's family for God's comfort. He called his wife after the prayer, and informed her of his safe return to the hotel.

After resting for an hour, he spent some hours working on his writing project. Eventually, he was grateful to God for enabling him to accomplish the project despite other engagements.

*

Early in the morning the next day, Nachau got set. He went to the receptionist and settled his bills. After saying goodbye to Anano, Tigana, and Goddy, he left the hotel anxious to reach home.

His journey was full of several thoughts, especially on the resistance of Felicia and Anano towards the gospel despite all that they had heard.

His comfort came from the fact that his role was to share the gospel, the Holy Spirit knows how best to convict and convert.

He did remember on his way to buy a special gift for his daughter and his son. He also bought a beautiful wristwatch for his wife.

His family received him well on his return.

CHAPTER 10

One night, Tigana could not sleep. She rolled restlessly on her bed, thinking. The question Nachau asked her on Jesus' love kept on ringing hard in her mind. All efforts to ignore the pressure were abortive.

Eventually, after a long struggle, she sat up on her bed, and started crying bitterly. The errors of her life stared at her for the first time.

Tigana knelt down in tears, and started praying to God for forgiveness. She prayed and wept so loudly that some of her neighbours overheard her. They started wondering what was wrong.

Anano, reluctantly, and hopeful that she could find a fault to use against Tigana, came and started knocking at Tigana's door.

Tigana did not open the door. She continued to pour her heart out to God, feeling more and more ashamed of her lifestyle.

After praying, she lay quietly on the floor in expectation. Suddenly, Tigana felt peace in her heart, of a kind that she had never experienced in her life. Her burden of guilt became light.

When she stood up, her face was full of smiles. Her environment began to irritate her for the first time.

Anano, once again, tried her luck and knocked at the door. Tigana went and opened it.

"I hope everything is okay with you?" Anano asked teasingly.

"I am okay, my friend," Tigana replied joyfully.

Anano was surprised to hear Tigana call her a friend, and responding in such a friendly manner. "Are you sure you are okay?"

"I am. I have just found the missing link in my life," Tigana replied.

"What is that?"

"Not what, but who. I just received Jesus as my Lord and Saviour," Tigana disclosed happily.

Anano burst into mocking laughter. She laughed to the point of tears." You are not serious! Have you ever heard of mixing Jesus with prostitution?"

"I am no more a prostitute."

"I don't believe you, until I see it in action."

"Please, forgive me for the bad ways I treated you."

Anano kept quiet, as she wondered on the reality of Tigana's new lifestyle.

"You too should respond to God's love, before it is too late," Tigana encouraged.

"I am not yet old. I will have pleasure first before any other thing."

"I hope time will wait for you."

"I assure you it will," Anano responded proudly.

"Thank you for your concern. I need to do something else if you wouldn't mind," Tigana said politely.

Anano did not utter a word. She walked away from Tigana to her room.

Tigana felt huge burden in her heart to tell more people, especially prostitutes, the gospel. She invited Marka and Rose to her room and shared her testimony of conversion with them. The way Tigana talked was abnormal. She addressed them with respect and love with tears in her eyes, as she shared the testimony of her conversion.

"Rose, forgive me for my wickedness. I deceived your parents and you. Please, find a place in your heart to forgive me. I don't deserve mercy from you," Tigana knelt down before Rose and cried bitterly.

Rose could not hold back her tears. She also cried as she listened to Tigana.

"Whatever action you take against me is right. I will take you back home and seek for forgiveness from your parents," Tigana said.

Marka looked at the situation in pity. She had also started feeling the guilt of sin in her heart. For the first time, she realized how bad their situation was. Tears also rolled down her cheek.

Rose had several thoughts on her mind. She had long wished to make Tigana pay bitterly one day for her wickedness. The condition of her mind suddenly had flow of mercy towards Tigana instead of hatred.

Eventually, both Marka and Rose knelt down and prayed to God for forgiveness of their sins. Peace overshadowed their hearts after the prayer. They hugged each other, shedding tears of joy.

*

Felicia was in the room with Murinji when suddenly police officers surrounded the hotel and brothel, dressed ready for battle.

The people in the hotel and brothel were confused. Five officers went into the compound of the prostitutes and ordered them out one after the other with main focus on Felicia's room. Murinji peeped through the window to know the reason for the noise. His mood changed to fear when he saw the police officers. Felicia also peeped through and felt the same fear.

Murinji rushed, picked his jacket and removed a pistol getting ready for a battle. He knew that he was the culprit the police were looking for after the series of robberies he had executed in the town recently.

"What are you doing," Felicia asked in fear.

"Shut up!" Murinji reacted. "They are looking for me; but I will never allow them to arrest me!"

"Why are they looking for you?" Felicia inquired anxiously.

"This is not the time for questions," Murinji replied, as he got prepared to escape.

Immediately he jumped out through the window leading to the backyard of the compound, two police officers noticed him. They shouted at him to surrender or they would fire at him. Murinji became stubborn and fired his pistol. In the gun battle, Murinji was shot and died on the spot.

Murinji had lived his life as a criminal, who enjoyed depriving people of their possessions. He and his gang members had been linked with the recent death of two wealthy men in the city in their efforts to rob them. The police had been trailing him since then.

Goddy, Felicia, the rest of the prostitutes and some male customers were arrested and taken to the police station for further investigation. The women were locked in a cell separate from the men.

While in the cell, Tigana engaged Felicia in a discussion.

"Accept my sympathy over the loss of Murinji," Tigana said, as she sat on the floor next to Felicia.

Felicia didn't reply. She was deep in thoughts.

"God is in control. He will free us from here," Tigana encouraged.

"What do you want?" Felicia reacted.

"I talked to you as a friend," Tigana replied politely.

"Don't listen to her pretence. She claims she has received Jesus as her Lord and Saviour," Anano said angrily.

Felicia became quiet for a short time. "Is it true that you have received Jesus?" she asked.

"It is true, my friend. I hope you will also consider making such a decision. It just occurred to me that just as we are now in a cell without freedom that is how we have been imprisoned by sin. We have really missed so much in life living as prostitutes. I have found my freedom, I am sure God wants you to find yours. Forgive me for the harsh ways I treated you," Tigana stated.

Felicia started crying. "I should have made the decision earlier, but I became stubborn. You are the last person I would expect to make such a decision. Did you have a discussion with Nachau?"

"Yes, I did," Tigana replied.

"No wonder you talked like this."

"Felicia, you knew full well that living as prostitutes can't lead us to a better life. God helped me to overcome my fear. He is willing to help you too," Tigana said.

"Since God changed you, I have no reason to remain stubborn."

"Think about it, please," Tigana emphasized.

After the discussion, Felicia, in tears, hugged Tigana, as she also prayed to God for forgiveness.

It was a moment of tears. Tigana used the opportunity to share her testimony. Kuyanga and two other prostitutes also received Jesus. Anano and others remained stubborn and laughed at them over their new experiences.

Felicia begged one of the police officers to use her cell phone, which was among the personal items collected from the suspects and call Nachau's number to enable her inform him of the development.

After receiving the news, Nachau and his wife drove to the town the next day and went to the police station where Felicia was jailed. They were sad to see their friends at the police station, but rejoiced over the testimonies of salvation they heard among them.

*

After some days in cells, the suspects were released. There was no evidence of their connection to Murinji's criminal acts. Nachau and Akio played vital roles in the process.

Goddy and others thanked them for their kindness.

Felicia, Tigana and other prostitutes that repented forsook prostitution. Anano remained stubborn despite further efforts by Felicia to help her have a new lifestyle. One day, on her way for a weekend, with one of her customers in a town 60 kilometres away from the brothel, they got involved in a motor accident and all of them died on the spot.

Anano's friends were moved with sadness over the news of her death. Her people were informed of the incident. They came and took the corpse to her village where it was buried. Nachau, Akio and Anano's friends attended the burial. Tigana and Felicia stayed behind in the village with the people of Anano for one extra day before leaving the village.

Goddy, also received Jesus. He stopped the prostitution and alcoholic aspects of his business. He introduced decency into his line of business.

Tigana went home with Rose, explained the truth behind her actions and asked for forgiveness from Rose's parents. It was a battle for Rose's parents to forgive. It took the intervention of the elders of the village before the matter was put to rest.

For some months, Nachau and his wife had encouraged Felicia, Tigana and their friends in God's Word. After that, Tigana and Felicia had a burden of starting a ministry to the prostitutes, which also involved advocacy against girl – child trafficking, helping victims discover a better life in Jesus. They named the ministry, 'GRACE.' Tigana became the first leader of the ministry.

Goddy donated the compound that the prostitutes had used in the past for prostitution, as his contribution to Grace Ministry. Nachau and his wife helped them furnish the compound.

As part of the ministry, they established a tailoring centre, where Felicia used her skills to train former prostitutes in self-reliance. It was also a source of income for the ministry in its evangelizing activities. The impact of their services was felt in different states, with many prostitutes giving up prostitution. Their ministry received great support from individuals, organizations and Church denominations.

As for Selemo, he repaired his motorcycle and continued with the business. He eventually started the saloon business, which became successful. Nachau had earlier supported him with some funds, besides the funds he had saved from his motorcycle-business. He employed three people to work for him in the saloon. God also blessed them with twin baby boys. They have also started a ministry of comfort to parents who have experienced loss of children. Many parents were encouraged by the grace of God.

Usilari became a professional hairdresser for their female customers. She had also worked in partnership with the ministry of Tigana and Felicia in training former prostitutes in hairdressing.

One day, Nachau received a note from Felicia and Tigana:

We decayed, and the odour of our lives was unattractive.
We were rejected, living in dustbins of
life and losing the fresh air outside it.
We were like oranges without juice.
Like horses with three legs.
Like cows awaiting the next day at an abattoir.
We waited in fear for each new day,
though pretending to be courageous.
Instead of death, we got life.
We know that we do not deserve to live, but all because of God's
grace, we have been transformed into instruments of blessings.
We thank you for your friendship, humility and love to us.
We join you as you often say, "To God be the glory."

Scriptural References

John
1:4, 2

Ephesians
4:18, 1

James
1:2-5, 105